Dear Reader,

A soothing cup of tea has long been one of my favorite comforts—a hug in a mug. Add my fascination for cozy spaces and international intrigue, and *Tea Rose* came alive for me before it actually was words on my computer screen. And I can definitely appreciate the excitement of a fresh start, of diving into new challenges as Jan, Elaine, and Rose did. These characters have pluck, lifelong doses of it, and for that reason alone they were delightful to me to get to know. I hope you'll find them to be just as delightful as I did. We're still early on in Tearoom Mysteries, and I hope you're looking forward to adventuring with them more over future volumes. God bless you and may all your teas be tasty.

Erin Keeley Marshall

Tearoom Mysteries

Tearoom for Two
Tea Rose

TEAROOM
mysteries

Tea Rose

ERIN KEELEY MARSHALL

Guideposts

New York

Tearoom Mysteries is a trademark of Guideposts

Published by Guideposts Books & Inspirational Media
110 William Street
New York, New York 10038
Guideposts.org

Acknowledgments

Cover and interior design by Müllerhaus
Cover illustration by Ross Jones, represented by Deborah Wolfe, Ltd.
Typeset by Aptara, Inc.

Printed and bound in the United States of America
10 9 8 7 6 5 4 3 2 1

Tea Rose

CHAPTER ONE

The next tea Rose and Elaine will serve to you is a personal favorite, the Russian Troika."

Jan Blake paused with a smile for the two dozen guests who had come to Tea for Two's first of two Saturday gatherings they were calling "Teas around the World." For an hour and a half that afternoon, the women had been introducing several teas from various cultures. And as always at Tea for Two, pastries were plentiful.

These events would help usher in the town of Lancaster's Fourth of July fest. Outside the three-story house that Jan and her cousin, Elaine Cook, had turned into a thriving business on the shore of Chickadee Lake, the earth had released its last hold on spring, and the heat of summer reigned over the sun-dappled waves beyond the windows of the shop. The air inside the cozy yet sophisticated space was scented with exotic spices and the buttery pastries that Jan turned out daily in the kitchen.

The tables scattered throughout the double parlor buzzed with chatter as Elaine and Rose, a local young woman they had hired to help them in the tearoom, placed a teapot on each table.

"You'll notice hints of bergamot, mandarin, and other orange varieties in this Russian black tea. The bergamot will be familiar from the China and Ceylon teas you tried a few minutes ago, but the other citruses make this one unique. When I think of Russia, I'm reminded of cold, harsh weather with snow piled high, so the warm tone of the citrus always is a pleasant surprise for my taste buds."

Several customers nodded as Jan gave them time to sample the drink and herself a chance to sneak a glance at the list in her waist sash. Rose was up next. She tucked the list back in its hiding place, then removed her blue-rimmed glasses to wipe the lenses. She breathed another quick prayer that Rose would be able to recite her part well.

Their first summer season had been eventful so far, and Jan knew the majority of the people sitting around her at least by name. Most had been strangers weeks ago but had become somewhat familiar to her, if not genuine friends, in that short time.

Many of the men, women, and even a few children in sun-dresses, shorts, and polo shirts had been regular visitors to Chickadee Lake for years; not quite locals, but summer regulars. Others were year-round residents, and Jan was thankful she would be able to enjoy their company long after the summer ended. She didn't much like good-byes.

Although a longtime resident of Central Maine herself, and a Lancaster resident when she was younger, Jan was really more of a newcomer to Chickadee Lake than many of them, and she felt like pinching herself that this dream business of Elaine's and hers had become a reality that was affording both widows a way to connect with this community.

Only a few of the afternoon's patrons remained unknown to her. Jan replaced her glasses, then watched Elaine and Rose mingle and chat with the guests about which of the teas were favorites and why.

She didn't recall ever seeing the distinguished older man sitting in the far corner of the larger east parlor, and she couldn't decide if his stern visage was off-putting or simply reserved. He seemed to keep to himself, even among his tablemates.

Jan also hadn't met the stylish couple who chatted pleasantly with Rue and Ned Maxwell at their table on the opposite side of the room. The Maxwells were in their thirties and owned the Northwoods Bed-and-Breakfast. Jan wondered if the woman with beautiful blue-black hair and her fair-skinned husband were staying at the B and B. Toned and well dressed, they looked like thirtysomethings fresh from the big city who could use some Chickadee Lake sunshine.

She made a mental note to introduce herself to all three newcomers before the event ended.

She glanced at her watch and saw that they were on schedule to wrap up the tasting session in the next fifteen minutes. It didn't seem possible after all the planning that it was nearly over already. At least they could do it all again the following Saturday.

Chickadee Lake's population had doubled when the summer season kicked off. The guest cottages, campsites, and bed-and-breakfasts were filled with vacationers on break from their off-season lives around the country. She caught bits of conversations about the chicken barbecue and corn boil the following weekend and plans for grilling and evening fishing after the tea.

She looked forward to the holiday hoopla; even all the preparation suited her because it built camaraderie in town and helped her feel a sense of belonging in her new home.

The past few weeks had been stressful and somewhat weighted by the recent death of Rose's mother. She welcomed a diversion for all three of them.

Elaine and Rose returned to Jan's side. "This has been a super idea." Elaine squeezed Jan's shoulder. "Great job, cousin."

"Well, shucks. Thank *you* for handling all the research and ordering the teas. It's been fun to discover new varieties and to learn some things I never knew that I never knew about our line of work."

Elaine's smile brightened her blue eyes even more. Like Jan, Elaine was in her midfifties. She still had only an occasional gray strand in her short brown hair. Elaine turned her attention to Rose and reached over to wrap an arm around the younger woman's shoulders. "And kudos to you for the ideas for our outfits, and for finding these getups."

"Yes, Rose," Jan added. "They've been so fun. I've always wanted to wear a sari but never had an opportunity until now. I love it."

The women often dressed in Victorian costumes when hosting, but for today they had agreed on Rose's suggestion to play up the cultural theme by donning period dress from the various countries represented by the teas. Jan wore a shimmering silver Indian sari of pure silk that flattered her petite frame; Elaine, somewhat taller, wore a traditional African tribal dress in a caramel color accented by blue, red, and yellow beading; and Rose looked classically German in a patterned red dress with crisscrossed lacing on the white bodice. Her wheat-colored braid draped over her shoulder and finished the charming look.

To the guests, Rose appeared as cheerful as ever today, but Jan noticed the slight strain in her features that gave away the extra effort of maintaining a lighthearted façade.

Rose caught Jan's glance and lifted her mouth in a smile.

Too quick, definitely forced. Jan leaned over and spoke quietly, "You're next, but if you're not up for this I'll cover for you if you'd like. I know you'll do great, but you've had a rough few weeks."

Rose rubbed her hands together. "Thanks, Jan, but I'm fine. Getting ready for this has been a good break from going through Mom's things."

"Our guests will love your tea, Rose," Elaine encouraged, "and especially the dessert. I'll bring in the pastry cart and the next tea cart while you introduce them."

"Thanks, Elaine." Rose smoothed her skirt, then stepped forward to address the room. Most of the guests had finished the Troika tea, and suntanned faces turned a few at a time until Rose had everyone's attention.

"Hi there. My name is Rose Young, and as many of you know, I've been working here for a while." She swallowed. "I'm happy to share with you a tea that's native to my heritage and also a German pastry I grew up eating."

A twinkle shone from Rose's blue eyes as she looked toward Jan. "Jan's been a great teacher in the kitchen, but she also agreed to let me talk about my family's recipe for apple *kuchen*."

Elaine and Jan began delivering plates of the dessert, and on a whim Jan headed toward the distinguished stranger in the back corner. As she set a plate in front of him, he straightened quickly and slipped a piece of paper underneath the table. Jan got the impression that he didn't want her to see it.

"Here you go, sir. Enjoy," she offered in a whisper.

When he didn't respond, she followed his gaze, which was trained directly on Rose.

"I don't believe we've met," she continued. "I'm Jan Blake, co-owner here. Is this your first time at Tea for Two?"

He cleared his throat and met Jan's gaze briefly before focusing on Rose once more. His eyes were a greenish hue, his hair dark gray, and he wore a green golf shirt and gold watch. Handsome but not necessarily welcoming, Jan decided.

"Kuchen is popular in Germany, and my mother learned to bake it as a child," Rose continued. From her skirt pocket she withdrew a worn recipe card and held it up.

"How well do you know that woman?" the man asked without looking at Jan, and not really as a question but more as a statement that expected an answer.

Rose went on. "Mom passed it down to me, and it seems fitting to share it with you all today." Emotion caught her voice.

Jan exchanged glances with Elaine, who was heading back to the dessert cart. She knew Elaine was also hoping that Rose's mention of her mother wouldn't undo her resolve.

Something about the man's question, and Rose's current vulnerability, sent a feeling of unease through Jan, and she chose her words carefully. "Rose has lived in the area all her life." Making sure she smiled, she added, "And what is your name, sir? Where are you from?"

The man lifted a hand off the table slightly, a dismissive gesture that made Jan want to frown. The woman sitting next to him raised her eyebrows, as if to say, "I can't figure him out either."

Jan left him and returned to the cart for more plates. She and Elaine continued delivering kuchen, followed by more teapots, each one unique.

As people tasted the apple pastry and sipped their drinks, Rose explained about the tea. "East Frisian tea, known as *Ostfriesen* in German, is a loose tea like the others you've tasted today. It comes from the northwestern part of Germany. Before you pour it into your teacups—or tea *glasses,* as they often are called in East Frisia—place a few of the rock candies from your saucer into the glass. These candy sugars are called *kluntjes.*

"You'll see from the menus on your tables that the word doesn't sound like it's spelled. It's pronounced 'KLOONT-yuhs.' You may already have noticed a similar thing with the word *kuchen.* We Americans would pronounce it 'KOO-chin,' but in Germany the word is pronounced 'KOO-khin.' Anyway, when you pour the tea over the kluntjes, listen as they crackle."

Around the room, guests lowered their ears close to their cups. Smiles lit their faces.

"Next, place a few drops of cream around the inside edge of your glass to make the clouds, which are another signature element of this drink. The dark copper blend of black, Assam,

Java, and Ceylon teas creates a malty and somewhat spicy character. Those ingredients mixed with the kluntjes and cream clouds feel like silk on the tongue." She paused for the guests to try their treats. Standing tall, she seemed composed.

She's doing well, Jan thought, but she knew Rose was grieving the loss of her mother as she spoke of her family connections to the tea and kuchen. What had been a source of love and happiness must be bittersweet now because Rose could no longer share these memories with her mom.

Elaine seemed to sense the underlying struggle too. "Rose and Jan have been holed up in the kitchen all week making the pastries on the table," she stepped up to explain, "but this one, I have to say, is extra special. Rose told me that the buttery cake base has coconut in it, and then it's topped with apple slices, an egg yolk and sour cream mixture, and finally cinnamon sugar. Then the whole thing is baked to perfection. It's heavenly, isn't it?"

As compliments erupted from all around, Rose lifted her head toward Elaine with a gentle smile. "Elaine is kind, and she is correct about the ingredients for the kuchen. Thank you for letting me share it with you." With that, she moved to stand next to Jan.

Jan placed a hand on Rose's back. "The East Frisian blend was our final sampling today. We hope you enjoyed it, along with the Indian teas, which were the Nimbu and Chai Hara. The Nimbu had the lemon-caramel flavor in a Darjeeling, and the Chai Hara was a green tea with cardamom, cinnamon, nutmeg, coriander, and ginger." She nodded to Elaine, who spoke next.

"We also gave you the African Red Bush, or *Rooibos*. It hails from South Africa and isn't a typical tea, but rather a medicinal herb that's harvested like a tea and is famous for its energy-boosting and antioxidant power."

Jan's turn again. "And then the China, Ceylon, Irish Breakfast, and Russian Troika teas. And finally, the East Frisian. Thank you for traveling the world with us from our lakeside tearoom. Who knew when you came to Central Maine that you would actually visit much more distant places?"

Chuckles followed, and a few chairs scuffed the floor as some people pushed back from the tables to leave. To Jan's dismay the stylish young couple and the stern older man all rose quickly and headed for the door. Several elderly women who were frequent customers had risen as well and were moving toward Jan, Elaine, and Rose. Jan knew she would miss her chance to meet the couple or find out more about the strange man. Resigned to the missed opportunity, she turned her attention back to her other customers and friends.

Rose excused herself quietly while Jan and Elaine visited up front with lingering customers and answered more questions about all things tea related. Priscilla Gates, the local librarian, and Bree Dickerson, the receptionist at the Lakeview Clinic, chatted at the counter while Elaine rang up their to-go bags of cookies.

Jan caught Rue's eye across the room and waved before heading back to the kitchen to get Rue's regular order of muffins for her guests.

"Cranberry-walnut, lemon poppyseed, and strawberry-cornbread this week," Jan said back up front as she handed the boxes to Rue. "I picked those strawberries fresh from Orchard Hill last week."

"*Mmm*, well, the boxes may be lighter by the time I get home! Ha!" Rue's blonde curls swung around the collar of her belted sundress.

"My lips are sealed." Jan smiled. "I was hoping to say hello to the couple sitting with you today, but they skedaddled quickly."

"Oh, the Tates? Yeah, they're fun. They've been with us a couple of days now. I don't know where they had to get to just now, but I think they're planning to stick around town a few weeks, so maybe they'll be back."

"Three dozen still good?" When Jan saw that her question didn't register with Rue, she clarified. "The muffins. Are three dozen still enough each week?"

"You know, I almost ordered more because we're booked through July, but instead I'm sending our guests directly here."

Jan and Elaine exchanged grins.

"Thanks, Rue!" Elaine spoke up from behind the counter as the register drawer chimed again.

Rue glanced at her husband, who was accepting change from Elaine for the muffin order, while she kept talking a mile a minute. "Or I bring them in myself. Lila and Ray—they're the Tates—they happened to be the lucky guests I talked into coming with me today. I'm all about drumming up business for each other."

She winked conspiratorially. "I was hoping to snag the entire Burgess clan because there are six of them, but they're out on the water all day. You've met them, right?"

Jan acknowledged that she'd met the Burgesses, a family with four teenagers from Des Moines, Iowa. "They've been in a couple of times." She was about to ask if the man in green happened to be staying at the B and B, but Ned finished at the counter and came to stand next to his wife.

"Jan was asking about our guests, hon." Rue wiped a crumb from his beard stubble.

"Uh-huh," Ned mumbled, leaning away from his wife's fingers. "She can't take me anywhere without cleaning me up."

Rue shot Jan a long-suffering smirk, rolled her eyes, and changed the subject. "I'll try to remember to bring in some groceries for the food drive in a day or two."

The register kept ringing as customers ended conversations and came up to choose treats from the glass display to take home. An hour later, the last ones had left and quiet mellowed the shop while the cousins wiped down tables and stacked the remaining dishes on the carts in the east parlor to take to Rose in the kitchen.

As they each pushed a cart that way, Rose emerged with her keys and purse. "Oh, I'm sorry. I guess I thought I got the last of it." She started to set down her things.

"No trouble," Elaine answered. "We can finish up. Why don't you go home and relax?"

"Absolutely," Jan agreed. "And thank you again, Rose … Are you sure you're okay?"

Rose blinked. "Thanks, you two. I'll be fine."

"Is there anything we can do for you? How are you doing sorting through your mother's things?"

To Jan's surprise, Rose lifted both hands to wipe the sudden rush of tears that had welled up.

"Rose?" Elaine questioned, moving close and pulling the woman into a hug. "What's going on?"

Rose cried for a few seconds before she collected herself and attempted to brush off the cousins' concerns. "I'm okay. At least I will be. I think." She looked from one employer to the other and her jaw dropped slightly, as if she couldn't find the right words.

They waited.

Rose shook her head quickly, as though she wanted to brush off something unpleasant. "I...It's just that I...Well, here, I'll just show you." She reached into her purse and removed a folded piece of parchment stationery. She opened it and looked at it as if it carried a disease, then shoved it toward Jan. "I found this in Mom's things last night."

Jan took the paper and studied it for several seconds. "It's a death certificate."

"Yes, it is," Rose whispered. "Read the name and dates."

Jan's heartbeat quickened and a leaden feeling weighted her body. "Tatiana Rose Schultz. Born June 6, 1990. Died November 17, 1991." Other than the names, the words were in a foreign language that Jan guessed to be German.

"Yes."

Jan looked from Rose to Elaine and back to Rose. She didn't want to think what she couldn't help but think.

Rose nodded slowly, her face flushing a deep red and more tears threatening to overflow. "Yes, my birthday is June 6, 1990. And I am Rose. Rose *Tatiana*. That death certificate is too close to be coincidence, Jan. It's mine."

CHAPTER TWO

Elaine scrambled to sort her thoughts as she followed Jan and Rose to the big kitchen at the back of the house.

The outside temperature had dropped enough to open a couple of kitchen windows and the door to the screened porch. Summer sounds floated inside on a breeze off the lake. A bird chirped from a nearby tree, and a boat motor purred in the distance. Shadows hung across the room, which had been remodeled in the spring to fit the needs of the tearoom. Late-afternoon light subdued the gleam of the commercial-grade appliances and granite countertops.

Jan pulled out a chair for Rose, then sat down with her at the round wooden table. Rose reached for the antique tin planter full of napkins and grabbed one to dab her eyes. Elaine went to the private bathroom nearby and came back with a tissue and sat down.

For a moment no one spoke while Rose held the tissue to her nose. The dots on the double wall ovens' digital clocks blinked the seconds while Elaine considered what to say. She reached across the table for the younger woman's hand.

"I can imagine how that certificate must have thrown you, Rose. You're sure it's yours?"

Rose nodded while she massaged the back of her neck with her free hand. "My last name is Young, but it used to be Sims. I don't know why it says Schultz, but I know it's mine."

Elaine could tell Jan felt as stuck as she did trying to sort through how a death certificate could exist for someone who was sitting across the table. "What makes you so sure? Obviously you're alive, so there's got to be some mistake. Could you have had a twin sister your mom never told you about? Or maybe a cousin born the same day as you? Actually, a cousin would explain the different last names." The suggestions seemed a little absurd to Elaine, but then so did the certificate.

Rose kept shaking her head. "I know the name doesn't match mine exactly, and I've run through all those possibilities. I know in my gut that it's mine, but it's more than that."

Once Rose's words started coming they flowed quickly.

"Obviously, there's some mistake because I'm not dead. But I always knew my mom was keeping a secret that had to do with me. Little things that didn't make sense. Like sometimes I'd walk into her room and she'd be in her closet and turn suddenly and put her hands behind her back as if she'd been looking at something she didn't want me to see. She'd make an excuse that she was looking over my Christmas list. But usually her eyes looked teary. Who cries over her daughter's wish list? I never could figure out what she wouldn't talk about, but it made me feel guilty that something about *me* was making her sad."

"Oh, Rose, no. I'm sure that wasn't true." Jan blinked back tears.

Elaine kept quiet for the moment. Rose's explanation still seemed like she was jumping to conclusions, even though her mother clearly had some kind of secret.

"I have one memory that makes me know the certificate is mine, even though I can't explain why it exists." Rose looked out the window, focused on something far away. "One of the pictures we had on the wall at home for a long time was of Mom, Dad, and me. I was about three and half."

She smiled and her voice dropped to a whisper as she looked at Elaine. "I loved that picture. I wore a necklace, a gold chain with a figure-eight pendant. Inside the two loops of the eight were my birthstones. Pearls for June. Dad has a matching tie tack, only his stones are diamonds. I have no idea where the picture is now, or the necklace for that matter. The necklace wasn't in my jewelry box as a child, and I didn't see it again until I was about fifteen, which was the last time I ever saw it."

A cat meowed softly outside. *Earl Grey must be back,* Elaine realized, *looking for a snack.*

"Dad and I had been away at a father-daughter camp weekend, but we came back early Sunday afternoon. Mom was asleep in their room when I found her, so I tiptoed in to cover her with a blanket. My old pendant was lying on her nightstand. It took me a second to recognize it from our picture. I'd never gotten a close look at it, but I did then. Etched on the back was the name *Tatiana Rose*, which was pretty confusing to me."

"Your name, but switched," Jan said.

"Yes. Why would Mom have my name switched—or not have the jeweler correct his mistake?" She rubbed her lips together. "She woke up right then, and when she saw it in my hand she nearly bolted out of bed. I didn't know what to make of her reaction back then, but looking back I can only say it was fear. She made some excuse about never getting around to correcting the mistake, and I never saw the necklace again. Sometime later I guess she took down the picture too, but I don't remember when that happened either."

She looked pointedly from Elaine to Jan. "There was no other necklace with 'Rose Tatiana' on it. There was no other Tatiana Rose. *I* was Tatiana Rose. Which means that I still am, but I don't understand how."

Elaine shook her head slowly, still considering possible explanations. "Have you asked your dad about it?"

Rose's father, Waterville orthodontist Dr. Clifton Young, owned the family house on the lake on the outskirts of Lancaster, nearly to Penzance. Rose had lived with her parents in the months since returning to Lancaster from Portland, Maine, after a stressful stint as a nurse had proven to her that health care was not her thing.

Now she was back in Lancaster for some breathing time to figure out what might be next. She had told Jan and Elaine that she hoped to help people in a different way, although she wasn't sure what that looked like for the future. For now, it was in the form of food service. In the short time the cousins had known Rose, her friendliness and attentive eye for whatever needed to be done made her a welcome addition for the cousins and their guests.

Unfortunately, shortly after Rose settled back in temporarily with her parents, her mother, Aliza Young, passed away unexpectedly from complications following heart bypass surgery. Rose was back to work two days after the funeral, and Elaine had noticed the quiet and somehow peaceful way Rose kept her grief at bay while she worked.

But this new information was very strange, and a little unsettling. Elaine hoped they would find a logical explanation for the bizarre certificate.

"I showed Dad the certificate last night," Rose said, "and he was as surprised as I was." A troubled look flitted across her face. "At least he seemed to be. He didn't have any real answers but just said we know she loved us, and everyone has things in their past they'd like to keep to themselves."

From the corner of her eye, Elaine saw Jan's head tilt in question. Clifton's answer must have sounded awkward and unsatisfying to her too.

Rose was shaking her head. "I don't even know how to process this. Mom's been gone only a few weeks. Dad and I are still working through that."

"Of course," Jan said, getting up to heat the copper tea-kettle. She pulled three flowered teacups from a cupboard and placed them on the table. She also brought a jar of honey from the pantry before waiting near the island while the tea-kettle heated.

"How's your dad doing?" Elaine asked.

Rose folded the parchment document and tucked it into her purse on the back of her chair. "Dad's been Dad. Quiet and steady. But I know he's hurting. He and Mom had their troubles, especially this past year. But they managed to work things out. He moved back into the house only a few months before she was scheduled for surgery. And then she didn't recover like we expected. I'm sad for him as much as for me, and I sometimes wonder if he might feel regret...or have guilt maybe...for whatever part he thinks he played in their issues."

"I'm glad for all of you that they reconciled," Jan said comfortingly. "It's easy to replay every mistake, especially after losing a loved one. That still gets me at times, and Peter's been gone a decade."

Elaine cleared her throat. "Clifton didn't say anything else?"

Rose ran her fingers over the table's distressed chestnut surface before looking up. "He kind of bluntly asked me to just leave it alone," she said. "I don't know what to make of that."

Jan wrinkled her nose.

"I asked him why, and after hemming and hawing a little, he said he wanted to wait a couple of weeks until after the election, when he could focus on it better."

Elaine tried to keep her face stoic. She didn't want to sound critical of Rose's father, but his request seemed pretty evasive.

"It made me wonder what he might know." Rose's words came out on a big exhale, and they echoed Elaine's thoughts. "I want to be understanding, but I can't help it. It bugged me that he didn't want to talk about it."

"Will you wait, as he asked?" Elaine ventured.

"I don't know. I don't know what this death certificate could possibly mean, but I feel like it will probably change... everything. You know? Everything I thought I knew about my life. And possibly about who my dad is." Rose's elbow rested on the table as she sank her head into her palm. "I'm just really confused."

A low whistle from the teakettle began to build in volume. Jan got up, took the kettle from the burner, and poured the near-boiling water over the tea leaves. Then she brought the teacups, brimming with soothing chamomile tea, to the table. She sat down with Elaine and Rose, and quiet hung in the room again while the hot drinks steeped.

Elaine rolled her shoulders and flexed her tired arms over her head. "Who knows? He might be more open to talking about it in a day or two." Privately, however, she agreed with Rose. It didn't seem fair for Clifton to make his grown daughter wait to discuss the situation, not when she had discovered such a confusing—not to mention disturbing—document, just because he was running for local office. But then again, he was also dealing with his wife's recent death. Maybe he was just trying to pace himself so he could handle the conflicting demands being placed on his time and emotions.

"Maybe so," Rose replied. "He does have a lot on his mind, and not just the election. Work's been really busy for him. And knowing him, he probably still thinks he needs to look out for me with everything going on. Daddy's little girl and all, even at twenty-six." Her smile was warm.

"Well, yeah," Elaine conceded. "Ben was always pretty protective of Sasha like that. Maybe your father doesn't know anything more but wants you to hold off until he can really look into the certificate with you."

"I've seen his campaign flyers and signs popping up around town," Jan said with a smile.

Clifton Young had entered the running for the selectman position in Lancaster after Roberta Thompson had to resign when her husband was transferred to Chicago. She had already moved, and Clifton was running against J. Eisley

Segouri, a transplant from Boston two years ago. Along with flyers and signs, discussions also were popping up as the election approached. Elaine sensed growing factions in the community about the men's differing visions for Lancaster's future.

"I know he'll be a great selectman," Rose said. "He's a good man." She took a deep breath. "I don't know if you knew this, but Dad adopted me. I was barely three years old."

Elaine felt her stomach get ready to growl and was glad when Jan spoke over it. "So your last name was Sims before that?"

"Yes. But I don't remember anything about that time. I don't remember the adoption. Dad and I tried several times over the years to get Mom to talk about her childhood. I don't know…maybe that's why I've always felt closer to Dad, even though he's my adoptive father."

The tea was hot on Elaine's tongue, but it was comforting for her tired nerves. "I didn't know your mother, but she must have confided in someone. Any idea whom she might have talked to?"

Rose shook her head as she ran a finger around the rim of her teacup. "She had a couple of friends, but mostly she was a homebody. She wasn't very social. I'll check, but I'd be very surprised if she'd told them anything."

"So it sounds as though this certificate might have been related to something that happened before your dad adopted you." Elaine bounced her tea bag in her tea a few times. "Your mom obviously knew the truth, but eventually you need to know how much she told him. How much he knows about your life with her before they got married."

"How'd your parents meet?" Jan asked.

Rose set her teacup on the table. "They told me, growing up, that they met while grocery shopping—they'd always smile and laugh a little about meeting so randomly. They dated for a month before getting engaged, then got married a week later—which would have been a year and a half after…after the certificate."

Rose seemed to struggle to say "*death* certificate." Elaine didn't blame her, considering Rose was clearly alive and well, though shaken.

Rose gave a slight laugh. "And they'd always end the story by saying it worked for them, but they joked that they had to be parental and tell me I wasn't allowed to do things so fast. I always teased them and said 'You mean do as I say, not as I do.'"

The cousins grinned.

Jan adjusted her sari's fabric over her shoulder. "Well, let's assume that story is true. It's probably best to give your dad the benefit of the doubt at this point, which may help when you ask him more about it." She glanced at the oven clock and stood. "Would you like to join us for supper?"

Rose sat up straighter. "Thanks, Jan, but I should get going. It's been a long day."

"Are you sure?" Elaine moved to get plates from the cupboard. "It *has* been a long day. Let us feed you, at least, since it doesn't look like this is a mystery we'll solve tonight."

Rose smiled again. "Okay. Deal."

Jan opened the commercial-size French-door refrigerator and pulled out a head of romaine lettuce and several other fresh vegetables before shouldering the door closed. "How does chef's salad sound? I have some grilled chicken left over from yesterday." She found a bag of baby peas in the freezer below, then nudged the drawer closed with her shoe.

"Sounds delicious. How can I help?"

"Why don't you get two or three eggs boiling?" Jan unloaded the vegetables on the island and pulled out the butcher-block cutting board beneath the granite countertop. "And then you can cut up the chicken while I fix the greens. It's on a plate on the top shelf. And there's also a package of bacon in the meat drawer."

"I can handle the bacon," Elaine interjected.

The women worked in companionable silence for a couple of minutes until Elaine spoke. "What do you know about your birth father, Rose?"

Rose sighed. "Not much. Which has always frustrated me. My childhood was great, but Mom never told me much about him. His name was Hans Sims. He was from Germany—what was West Germany then—but he was becoming a United States citizen when he and Mom were married. And then he died in a work accident." She grimaced. "He fell from scaffolding on a construction project."

"How awful!" Jan stopped dicing celery for a moment.

"I know. A couple of years ago I tried to find out more about him, but I ran into dead ends and then got sidetracked with work. Looking back, I always thought it was strange— Mom never seemed too sad about it."

"I guess everyone deals with grief differently," Elaine said while she laid out strips of bacon on the long griddle. Sizzling sounds were followed by the heady scent of meat cooking. "Aliza had obviously found happiness with your dad. Maybe she didn't want to dwell on the past."

"Maybe. But that certificate makes it pretty obvious that she purposely held more back from me than I realized. I'm not sure whether to feel hurt or angry or confused or excited to learn more about her or…"

"All of the above?" Jan bumped shoulders gently with her employee.

"Exactly," Rose said with a smile.

They finished preparing the light supper and sat down to eat. Elaine laid her napkin in her lap and offered to pray. She thanked God for the food and asked Him to guide their conversation. "Hold Rose close and help her trust You to walk this path with her."

When they'd said their amens, Jan spoke. "You know, Rose, we're here to help you." Rose was looking more refreshed with a plate of food in front of her. Elaine never ceased to be amazed at how good food, lovingly offered, could comfort and strengthen.

"That means a lot," Rose said. "It's already been tough to sort through Mom's things, but now my feelings are all over the place. Dad offered to help before this came up, but he's really busy with the campaign. I may hold off a while before bringing up the certificate again, but I can't sit around and do nothing either. I'd love your help going through some of her things."

"Well, we're happy to help." Elaine poked her fork into a cherry tomato. "Tomorrow is busy with church and Jan's family and my mom coming for lunch, but maybe Monday morning, before the tearoom opens?"

Rose agreed to that plan. "I know of at least one more box I haven't gone through yet, but I don't really know if that is all of it. Dad usually leaves for the clinic around seven each morning. Would you want to come by around seven fifteen?"

The cousins agreed.

"Allie, our renter, will probably still be home in our garage apartment, so please park so her car isn't blocked in. Hers is the yellow Beetle. She leaves for work around nine on Mondays."

"Got it." Jan said.

Rose perked up. "You know, I'm sort of excited at the chance to find answers about my mom. I never doubted she loved me. She was a great mom, and I miss her so much. As weird as it was to find that thing, maybe getting to the bottom of the certificate will help me understand her better."

"I bet it will," Jan said warmly.

They were almost finished eating. Elaine noticed Rose stifle a yawn, and she herself felt the day settle into her muscles. It was time to call it a night. She moved her empty plate aside and folded her arms on the table. "I know we're all tired, but here's one last idea for tonight. What if you were to show the certificate to a documents expert? I'm sure someone like that could at least give you some insight into it."

Rose wiped her mouth. "That's a good idea. I'll look into it."

"Actually," Elaine said, "one of my friends is an auctioneer. He might know someone. And I'm planning to see him tomorrow."

"Oh yes!" Jan agreed. "Showing it to Nathan is a great idea."

Rose swallowed a final bite. "Why don't you go ahead and ask him, if you wouldn't mind. I'll figure out when to talk to Dad."

After convincing Rose to let them clean up without her, Elaine and Jan boxed up two servings of kuchen and walked her down to her Honda CRV in the driveway.

Elaine squeezed Rose's shoulders. "Let us know if you need anything, okay?"

Rose nodded, then adjusted her German dress to get in the driver's seat.

The cousins waved as Rose started the engine. Gravel popped and crunched under the tires as the car left the driveway and disappeared down the street.

Elaine and Jan looked at each other, eyes wide.

"Wow," Jan said, releasing a breath. "That was definitely a shock. I know it would have been for me."

Elaine gave a sympathetic nod. "I don't know what she's headed for, but I think she has more surprises coming."

A distant *boom* of someone's fireworks practice rang out in confirmation.

CHAPTER THREE

The Sunday-morning sun seeped in through the screens on the back porch, where Jan curled up in a cushioned chair with her Bible, a hot mug of English breakfast tea, and one of her own miniature maple croissants. Looking out through the screen, Jan watched a pair of fishermen on the lakeshore, casting and slowly reeling, then casting again like a peaceful ballet. Soon one of the men strained with the pole; he reeled and a minute later he leaned down and pulled a flopping fish out of the water.

An early riser, Jan had already showered and dressed for church in a flowing jersey print skirt that brushed her ankles and a sleeveless, button-down shirt in a soft shade of butter that she'd knotted at her waist. An hour ago, round cubic zirconia stud earrings had sparkled back at her from her bathroom mirror as she tucked a dark curl around her ear and gave her outfit a final check before heading downstairs.

A batch of cinnamon-raisin muffins was baking in the oven, and she'd fed Earl Grey, the long-haired gray stray cat that had adopted them and now sat licking his paws outside the porch. Due to state health regulations he was not allowed in the house, but Jan and Elaine still enjoyed their business's furry mascot. He appeared several mornings a week for food, disappeared when he felt like it, and reappeared to charm the customers as they arrived.

She took another sip of the warm tea. She loved this porch with its wicker chairs, reclaimed wood side tables, ceiling fan, and woven indoor-outdoor rug. Elaine had found a small, galvanized-steel tub at Mainely Bargains Flea Market in Waterville, and they had loaded it with Jan's *Popular Science* magazines and recent issues of the *Penzance Courier,* the *Morning Sentinel,* and the *Weekly Wave,* and placed it on the plank floor next to one of the chairs.

The screened porch ran along one side of the house and wrapped around the entire front. Rocking chairs and several tables dotted the side porch for customers who preferred out-door seating.

She loved this home. It was larger than the one she'd shared with Peter and their kids, but it wasn't just the roomi-ness that pulled her in. Its rich wood floors and architectural trim, the curved staircase, large windows, stone fireplace, bay windows, beautiful parlors, gourmet kitchen, and their grand-mother's Nanking teapots displayed in the corner cupboard in the west parlor—all these qualities plus the house's Victorian aura made it feel like *home* deep down.

And the hints of mystery they'd discovered in the short time they'd owned the place only added to her fascination—namely, an old stovepipe flue cover that had been covered in wallpaper to match the wall, as was the custom, between the office and kitchen. During renovations, their electrician had discovered, behind the wall, a small box containing a valuable sapphire ring that had been dropped down the hole for the stovepipe many years earlier. The stove was long gone, of course, and if it hadn't been for the renovations, she and Elaine might never have known there had even been a hole in the wall at one time, much less a mysterious ring hidden behind it. Despite the challenges of running the tearoom and still getting settled in to life in Lancaster, Jan was fascinated by the ring, and she was determined to learn more about it—not just about the ring itself, but who might have put it there and why. Its story was waiting to be told.

She loved starting her own business with Elaine and seeing it grow. It was hard work, and at times she doubted herself, but mostly she felt recharged by it. She was making friends in Lancaster, and its small-town charms meant even more to her as an adult than she remembered as a child growing up there.

She let her gaze roam down their backyard to the lower deck and chairs, out to their dock, and over the acres of waves, whose colors were gradually lightening as the sun climbed higher.

Then her thoughts shifted to Rose. In one of the houses on the opposite shore, Rose and Clifton were probably waking up. Jan couldn't imagine how she would feel if she came across her own death certificate. It was so bizarre, and a little creepy.

Speaking of creepy, an image of the mysterious stranger in the tearoom yesterday crossed Jan's mind, bringing with it a sense of protectiveness toward Rose. In the short time she'd known Rose, she'd come to admire the younger woman's inner strength and helpful attitude. Jan breathed a prayer that they'd get to the bottom of that death certificate without too much upset to her. And she hoped Rose and Clifton could find their way together.

Jan and her children had struggled after Peter's death. They'd managed to figure out a new normal, but it hadn't been easy. Loss inevitably reconfigured things, but blessings could show up even in heartache.

A memory surfaced, surprising her. It was the morning of the baby dedication of her second granddaughter, Kelly, at church. Peter had been gone for a year, and Brian was feeling his father's absence strongly. As Jan watched him hold his tiny daughter before the service started, Elaine and her husband, Ben, surprised all of them and slipped into the pew beside them. They joined Jan's family up near the pulpit, committing to support Brian and Paula in raising Kelly to know God's truth and love. When the group went back to Brian and Paula's house for lunch, Jan saw Ben pull Brian aside. The two men talked for a while, and then Ben wrapped Brian in a fatherly bear hug. God had been faithful to make sure Ben and Elaine were on a brief leave in the States for that meaningful event in Jan's son's life.

Now Elaine was adjusting after Ben's death. She seemed to be doing well overall, and Jan prayed that would be the reality for the Youngs too.

Just then Elaine stepped on to the screened porch, pulling Jan from her reverie. "Hey there. Enjoying the peaceful morning?"

"You know me. One of my favorite times of day." Jan pushed up her glasses and smiled at her upbeat cousin.

Elaine had dressed for church in white silk capris and matching boatneck tunic. The straps of a cornflower-blue shell peeked out at her shoulders. She'd pulled her brown hair back with a length of printed silk like a headband. Silver flip-flops and hoop earrings completed her summery look.

"About our family lunch today," Elaine said, checking her left earring. "We can add more greens to last night's salad. No one will be the wiser. And I'll help put together the lasagnas before church." Elaine could cook, but the kitchen was more Jan's territory, whereas Elaine spent more time in the adjoining office doing billing and paperwork for the business, a partnership that worked well for them.

"I think we have enough time for that." Jan checked the clock on her phone as she slid her feet into her leather sandals nearby. She followed Elaine into the kitchen and deposited her Bible and empty tea mug next to the bowl of lemons on the counter.

The room smelled as though it had been doused with cinnamon. With only thirty seconds left on the timer, Jan turned off the upper of the two wall ovens and slipped on an oven mitt. Heat and a heady sweet aroma radiated off the muffin pan as she pulled it from the oven. "Still planning to talk with Nathan at church?"

"Yes, but I won't tell him many specifics. Just set up a time to talk later. Wow, those smell good."

Jan turned a knob on their range and watched as it poofed into life and began to burn steadily. She adjusted the heat and placed a wide, shallow stainless steel pan on the burner. Soon ground beef and Italian sausage were sizzling in it. Elaine hauled a large stockpot she had filled with water on to another burner and set the heat to high. Together they mixed sauce with spices, ricotta cheese, and other ingredients.

As Jan used a wooden spoon to break up some of the larger meat chunks, she glanced up to see a thoughtful expression on her cousin's face. "Thinking about Rose?"

Her cousin smiled and nodded. "Yes. Poor thing."

"I haven't stopped thinking about her either."

Elaine eased a muffin from the pan and pulled off a bite-sized piece. "Last night I lay in bed for nearly an hour trying to come up with an explanation for that death certificate." She popped the bite into her mouth.

"Me too. She didn't come right out and say it, but I got the feeling Rose might think her dad wasn't entirely surprised by it."

"You think he knows more than he's telling her."

"It seems likely, doesn't it?"

Elaine nodded. "But why would he keep anything from her? Rose is a grown woman. And a strong one. She might not like hearing some things about her mother, but leaving her hanging for two weeks until the election is over is maddening. I understand Clifton's ambition, and I even applaud him for it. But not at the expense of his daughter's well-being."

"Well, like you said, Rose is a strong woman. And hopefully he'll come around soon." Jan looked up from the sizzling meat in the pan, adjusted the flame slightly, and leaned against the counter. "Do you think there's a chance he's covering for something bigger, illegal maybe?"

"Covering for something that Aliza might have done? Who knows? I mean, that seems a stretch to me. But we have to consider the possibility that Clifton Young may have his own secrets he'd rather not make public." Elaine finished her muffin, then emptied two boxes of lasagna noodles into the boiling water, added a good amount of salt, and gave it a stir. "Especially right now."

"And if he doesn't know any more than Rose does, both of them will have more to discover together about Aliza."

"And they will," Elaine spoke confidently.

Jan thought for a moment. "The death certificate is bizarre enough on its own, but based on what Rose told us last night, the time frame makes even less sense," Jan ventured. She tried to organize the details on her fingers. "First: Rose has two sets of parents, Hans and Aliza Sims and Clifton and Aliza Young. Second: At some point between the two relationships, a baby girl allegedly died. Third: We don't know why there's a record of her death, why Aliza never told her about it, how the baby girl was related to Rose, or whether Hans or Clifton knew about it. I want to ask Rose if Aliza ever mentioned when and where she and Hans were married."

Elaine frowned. "Or if they actually *were* married. And then there's the last name Schultz that Rose doesn't understand. I wonder if she knows many relatives on her mom's side. Maybe one of them knows something more."

Jan was definitely confused on Rose's behalf. "The few times Clifton Young has been in here he's struck me as a salt-of-the-earth type, not someone who's hiding things. But if he isn't as honest as we think, I wouldn't feel very good voting for him."

"The death certificate would be just the thing for J. Eisley Segouri to make a big deal out of—to use as a smear tactic—even just as a distraction from Clifton's credentials." Elaine closed the door of the upper cupboard that held the spice jars. "Although we've had a good start with the tearoom, higher taxes worry me a little. And if other businesses are forced to close, we could lose customers too."

Jan's stomach did a little flip over Elaine's comment. She knew it was true. They wanted Clifton to win, not only because he was Rose's father, but also because he would fight for the qualities that made the Chickadee Lake area the charming place it always had been. But she shared Elaine's surprise over the growing number of residents who wanted to bring more trendy conveniences to Lancaster. Segouri's proposed location of a discount superstore was within sight from the third floor of their house.

But there was still more about Rose she hadn't run by Elaine. "Did you happen to notice that older man sitting at the back of the parlor yesterday?"

"You mean the one who wouldn't talk to you and left abruptly?" Elaine picked a crumb from the island and flicked it into the sink.

"One and the same."

"Yeah. He didn't seem friendly."

"He wasn't," Jan agreed. "But it was more than that. He specifically asked about Rose."

"Really? That's odd. What did he want to know?"

"He asked how well I know her. But then he wouldn't offer anything about himself. He was looking at her really intently. It was strange." When Elaine didn't say anything right away, Jan began to doubt her instincts. "I don't know. I'm probably being an alarmist."

"Did you mention it to Rose?" Elaine's forehead creased with concern.

Jan shook her head. "No, and I'm glad now that I didn't. Not given the recent circumstances. And Rose didn't say anything about him either. We can ask Rose whether she's seen him before."

Jan turned back to the stove. "Well, let's get this food done. We're about out of time."

They finished assembling two pans of lasagna, which they put into the refrigerator to await their return from church. As the first peals of the bells from Lancaster Community Church rang out over the town, the cousins hurried to Jan's old blue Camry for the short drive to the service.

THERE WERE TWO places left in a back pew as the pianist struck the first notes of "Great Is Thy Faithfulness." While she sang the familiar old hymn, Elaine noticed several townspeople in the congregation. First she spied the Maxwells, who were regular attenders. Then she noted that Russell and Kit Edmonds and their six-year-old daughter, Marcella, were there—Russell was the summer marine postman and a volunteer firefighter, Kit an elementary-school teacher. Also attending were Gavin and Annie Richardson and their three preteen and teenaged kids, Dori, Joe, and Ella. The Richardsons owned a dairy farm. Gavin's father, Ethan Richardson, lived with them as well, but Elaine didn't see him that morning. She would miss hearing his weather predictions.

Elaine caught Marcella Edmonds's wave before they both turned their attention back to the music. She smiled at the sight of the little girl's ponytail swinging with the tempo, and her heart lifted at the thought of her own grandkids, Lucy and Micah, who lived in Ohio. She wished her grandchildren could be there today. At least she would get to spend the afternoon with Jan's.

After the service, Elaine wove her way up front, where her friend Nathan Culver stood talking with Pastor Mike Ryder and his wife, Sarah.

Nathan's gray short-sleeved shirt matched the gray streaks running through his brown hair, but privately Elaine thought that the sprinkling of silver gave him a distinguished air. At fifty-eight, he still was lean and fit. His father and Elaine's father had been friends, so they'd known each other a long time, and Elaine was enjoying the resumption of their friendship. She'd always liked his easygoing nature. Although Nathan lived in Waterville, for the past couple of months he'd been attending church more frequently at Lancaster Community.

Nathan and the Ryders greeted Elaine warmly, and Sarah gave her hand a squeeze. "Great to see you. I wanted to come by yesterday for the tea but got caught up at home."

Elaine smiled. "We had a good time. You know there's another Teas around the World event next Saturday?"

Sarah nodded. "Yep, it's on my calendar."

The Ryders moved off to mingle with other congregants and Nathan turned to focus on her. "How've you been?" he asked amiably.

"Good." Elaine returned his smile. "I actually have a question for you, for a friend."

Nathan cocked his head. "What's up?"

"Well, she gave me permission to ask you about a document she found in her home. I'd like to explain it some other time. It's a little personal for her."

"My afternoon's pretty open, except for yard work."

Elaine told him of her plans for a family gathering. "But I could call you this evening."

"Yeah, no problem. You've got my number."

They talked about Nathan's work as they headed to the foyer, where Jan was talking with Bob Claybrook, an old school friend, as well as Rose, and Clifton, Rose's father. Elaine noticed the sparkle in Jan's eyes that was becoming habit whenever she was near Bob, and he seemed attentive to her as well.

Casually dressed in khakis, blue dress shirt and tie, Clifton was attractive, with average height and build. He was completely bald, with a full mustache and beard that were prematurely white. A silver antique tie tack in the shape of a horizontal number eight held two diamonds in the number's loops.

The tie tack that matched Rose's childhood pendant. It had to be.

"What a unique piece." Elaine motioned to the tack.

When Clifton looked down and held up the end of his tie, Elaine snuck a glance at Rose. Rose looked relaxed but shook her head almost imperceptibly, which Elaine took to mean she hadn't said anything more to Clifton about the death certificate.

"Thank you. A wedding gift from Aliza a long time ago."

"He's worn it to church every Sunday for as long as I can remember," Rose said affectionately. "I just wish I still had my necklace that matched it."

Clifton turned a curious look toward his daughter.

"Do you remember it, Dad? That one in our old family picture. Whatever happened to that?"

There was no missing the recognition on her father's face.

CHAPTER FOUR

Jan ran the knife's serrated edge through the last slice of a french loaf she was turning into garlic bread. Elaine had set the dining room table and was buttering the slices next to her at the island.

The windows and doors were closed to keep the house cool, but Jan could still hear the muffled sound of tires on gravel as a car pulled up outside. She heard car doors shut and the slap of shoes on the path from the driveway to the porch steps.

Elaine smirked. "Those sound like Max and Riley feet to me."

Two seconds later a pair of brunette heads popped into view. "Hey, Grandma! Let us in."

Smiling, Jan opened the screen door and greeted her five-year-old twin grandsons as they launched themselves at her and threw their arms around her waist. "What are you two doing here? Have you come to eat all my food again?"

They released each other, and she placed a hand on each boy's face.

"Yep," Riley stated. "I'm starving."

"Not *all* of it," Max corrected. "But probably most!"

Jan's middle child, Amy, and her husband, Van Kincaid, stepped into the kitchen with the breathless good-natured air of parents who keep up with kindergarten boys every day. Amy toted a bowl covered in foil.

"Hi there, Elaine," bright-faced, blonde-haired Amy greeted her. "Good to see you."

Elaine returned Amy's hug as she took the serving dish from her and put it on the kitchen table.

"That's my famous broccoli gratin," Van said with a wink.

"He's been in the kitchen more lately than I have," Amy added. "I love it." It was well known in the family that Amy was not a fan of cooking.

Brown-haired Van hugged Jan's shoulders. "Just trying to impress the best," he teased.

Their boys ran out of the kitchen through the east parlor as their father called out a reminder about using inside voices and behavior.

Jan smirked. "I'm sure they'll be fine and won't get into trouble."

"Heh!" Van chortled. "I wish I had your confidence."

"Maybe some of us can take them down to search for rocks on the shoreline after lunch. Speaking of eating, the lasagnas should be done within the hour, so we have a little time for the others to get here and for the food to finish."

As she spoke, two more engines rumbled in the driveway, and soon slender Tara, Jan's youngest, entered with a round of hellos and a tray of cut fruit. As usual, her eclectic jewelry complemented her outfit.

"Tara, you made that set, didn't you?" Elaine reached out to touch the turquoise and silver necklace. Matching earrings dangled from her ears, and a coordinating leather wrap bracelet had similar stones.

"I did. It's part of my new line for fall." After working for a retail jewelry chain for five years, twenty-seven-year-old Tara was designing her own pieces, selling them online and in stores, with hopes of including some shops in Lancaster before long. Jan enjoyed sharing budding entrepreneurial stories with her single daughter.

Tara smoothed a light-brown curl into place in her low side bun, and Jan felt a familiar skip in her heart at having her kids in her new home, even though none of the three had ever lived in the lake house.

Next through the door came Elaine's mother, Virginia Willard, who had ridden from Augusta with Brian and his family. Still independent at seventy-six, Virginia was aging gracefully, hair and clothing always styled well, making her seem younger than her age despite a gait that was slowing at a near-imperceptible pace. A few wrinkles wreathed Virginia's face when she kissed her girl. "Hello, dear."

Elaine helped her settle on to a kitchen chair as the final visitors came through the door—Jan's daughter-in-law, Paula, and two granddaughters, eleven-year-old Avery and nine-year-old Kelly, followed by her oldest child and only son, Brian. Chatter filled the porch and kitchen as the adults shuffled dishes on to the island and into the oven and refrigerator, and then poured drinks.

Standing next to Paula, Jan watched the girls run off to find their cousins, Avery with dark blonde hair like her mother's,

Kelly with dark hair and eyes like Brian's. "One minute little women, the next still young girls, aren't they?"

"It's hard to know which one we'll get from hour to hour," their mother joked.

Paula was good for Brian, Jan thought. She was upbeat like Elaine, which her overly serious son needed. "I remember those days of drama with my kids."

Brian joined Jan and Paula near the doorway that led into the east parlor. "So, Mom, what's the mood of the selectmen campaign these days?"

Jan turned toward him. "It seems to be getting more intense...and divided." The reference to the selectmen reminded her of Rose. How she hoped Rose and Clifton would talk honestly soon. Rose's comment in church about her necklace had obviously caught Clifton off guard, but after a moment he'd responded that he didn't have any idea what had happened to it.

"The election's only a couple of weeks away now," Elaine added. "Roberta already resigned and moved with her husband to Chicago. Clifton Young is the father of our server, Rose."

Virginia spoke up. "I read last week in the *Kennebec Journal* that his opponent is a Boston man."

"Old J. Eisley Segouri," Van nearly groaned, "and don't ever drop the *J*. He *will* correct you." He looked around at the questioning faces. "He banks with us." Van was a vice president of a bank in Augusta.

"I take it you don't much like him, Van?" Tara piped up, drawing grins from a couple of the others.

Van raised his glass in mock defense. "I didn't say that."

They waited for him to explain more, but he just gave them an inscrutable smile and said nothing.

Elaine took a seat across from Virginia. "I might know what you're trying not to say, Van. I was at the general store a few days ago when he was there, and he made a show of going on about his qualifications. Real estate developer, school board official, yadda yadda."

Paula sipped her water. "If I lived here I wouldn't be excited about his plans."

"I'm surprised so many people are excited about a super-store," Jan said. "I suppose it's why the Lancaster election is making the bigger papers."

"Did I hear that he wants to call it Seg-Way, after himself?" Amy asked, looking disappointed.

Tara looked up from doing a search on her phone. "Yeah, Amy. Maybe this is the article you read, Virginia. It calls Seg-Way 'the perfect one-stop segue for local folk and visitors to stock up before heading out for outdoor fun.'"

"That's the one." Virginia's silver head bobbed animatedly. "'Folk'—got to love that."

Just then the four kids came back into the kitchen. "When do we eat?" Max asked.

"Five minutes." Jan tousled his hair. "You kids wash up, and we'll pour your drinks."

"Grandma, do you ever play on the top floor?" Riley chimed in.

"I don't get up there much during playtime, Ri," Jan kidded.

Kelly shuffled for a spot in front of Jan. "It's so cool up there, Grandma."

And then all four kids were talking over each other until Amy raised her hands to signal one at a time.

Avery, the oldest, put on her voice of authority. "It's awesome. We could see way across the lake from up there."

They'd been so busy setting up the lower two levels of the house to run their business and to live that neither Jan nor Elaine had done much more than peek at the third floor and the tower room in the weeks since they'd moved in.

The oven timer buzzed. Adults scooted the kids toward the powder room to wash hands, while others carried food dishes into the dining room.

For all the work and time that went into preparing dinner, it disappeared quickly as the conversation turned to the upcoming Fourth of July celebrations on Chickadee Lake. The holiday was the following Monday, eight days away, and the kids fought to announce which activities they were most excited about. The first of the month was Friday, and that night would kick off with a chicken barbecue and corn boil, then four days of sidewalk sales in town, a farmers' market on Saturday and Sunday, the food drive Elaine was in charge of, the second Teas around the World next Saturday, drama skits by the Old Grange theater troupe, and of course fireworks on Monday night. Dozens of boats would be lit up out on the water while the sky erupted with color.

The kids finished eating quickly, so the boys and Kelly ran off to play and Avery went outside to visit Earl Grey, who had shown up at mealtime for a snack. The adults enjoyed a few quieter minutes at the table.

"Mom and Elaine," Tara began, "have you learned anything more about that ring you found?"

Elaine added more dressing to her salad. "Not yet. It's still in the safe-deposit box at the bank."

No one could imagine why someone might have dropped such a valuable gem down a flue pipe hole.

When the last piece of lasagna was finished, the adults took glasses of lemonade out to the front porch to visit more. As Tara was pointing out stores along Main Street that might be options for selling her jewelry, a shriek rang out from the depths of the house.

All the adults except Virginia bolted back inside and followed the sounds of chaos to the office, where Avery stood in the doorway looking horrified and pointing to the three younger kids.

"What in the world is going on?" Brian scolded.

The twins and Kelly looked guilty and confused holding large pieces of old wallpaper. Long vertical sections of it had been stripped off the office walls.

"We were just helping, Grandma," Kelly nearly whispered.

"Yeah, it was comin' off already!" Max declared.

Riley nodded vigorously.

The four parents looked stern, but Elaine stepped into the room. "You know, you're right, kids. It was starting to come off in a couple of places. That's a mighty big job you helped us with." She gave an encouraging look to the other adults, obviously hoping they'd go easy on the kids, whose hearts were in the right place.

Jan slipped around Brian and stood next to the boys and placed a hand on Kelly's shoulder. The girl looked like she was about to cry. "You all did help. We were planning to repaint this room anyway, right, Elaine?"

"Oh yes, we were."

Amy rubbed her lips together, and Paula held a fist to her mouth while she cleared her throat. Van and Brian looked dubiously at Jan and Elaine.

But Jan and Elaine held their ground. "It might be a good idea to ask before taking on such a big job next time, kiddos. But no harm done." Elaine reached over to mess with the boys' hair. Jan pulled Kelly close.

Still not looking convinced, Van and Brian offered to repaint the room themselves that week. "Just let us know the color and we'll pick it up at the store," Van offered.

Jan and Elaine agreed, and then, wanting to divert the attention away from the mess, Jan suggested they all go down to the shore after they cleaned up the office.

Soon the incident was behind them and Amy and Brian were showing the twins how to skip rocks. Max skipped one three times, and the little boy fist-pumped the air.

The sun's rays twinkled on the waves. Jan tilted her head to catch the warmth on her face. Some people might wrinkle their noses at the scents of marine life and wet soil that went along with living by water, but she'd choose nature's odors to smog and pollution any day.

A pair of birds soared on a wind gust high overhead. Down the shore to the west, small watercraft, cabin cruisers, and two party pontoons rocked gently in their slips at the marina. Across the lake, trees filled in the land as it rose back out of the water. Several houses peeked out from the greenery.

Jan wrapped the hem of her long skirt around her and held it at her knees. She slipped her feet out of her sandals and waded ankle-deep into the water, letting the concerns of the weekend wash away. Sand and small rocks pushed against the bottoms of her feet, and plant life tickled her toes. She trailed the fingers of her free hand through the cool water, and a family of minnows skimmed away from her.

"Grandma, what are you doing?" Riley hollered. Hands on his hips, he was all authority.

"Caught me!" Jan giggled and held back the urge to splash him.

Pretty soon several others followed her lead, with parents calling instructions to their young ones not to get too wet.

After twenty minutes, most of the group moved to the house's lower deck, where they visited at the white wrought iron table and garden chairs for another hour. Eventually the relatives left, and after Jan and Elaine had changed into comfy shorts and T-shirts, they sank on to Jan's soft blue couch in their upstairs sitting room.

Elaine propped her feet on the ottoman. "I'm spent. I love your kids and grandkids"—she stretched her arms over her head—"but they always make me miss mine."

"Hopefully Jared's family and Sasha can visit soon. I miss them too."

Elaine's cell phone chirped. Jan could hear enough to know Nathan Culver was the caller. Elaine moved to the hallway to talk, and Jan rested her head against the back of the couch. She pulled a throw pillow close and wrapped her arms over it. The scratchy old braided rug massaged her bare feet while she waited.

The entire second level was their private living space. Besides this room, each cousin had her own bedroom and bathroom. They also had a guest room and a craft room. Most evenings she and Elaine unwound up here before bed. The majority of the furniture had been hers because Elaine had learned to live sparingly in the decades she'd been married to Ben, who had retired as a lieutenant colonel in the army not long before he died of a heart attack. Jan knew that Elaine and Ben had talked about opening a bed-and-breakfast, but after he died, that dream had morphed into the tearoom business. Since Ben could no longer join her in the venture, Elaine had been happy to have Jan as a partner instead, especially since Jan couldn't imagine taking on the risk without Elaine.

Absentmindedly, Jan looked around the spacious room. They'd put Elaine's desk in the office, but there was plenty of space in the sitting room for Jan's desk. A bookcase against one wall held more of her science books as well as Elaine's tea references and fiction collection. Besides her couch, a couple of upholstered chairs they'd bought inexpensively provided seating, as did their grandmother's rocking chair that Jan figured had been in the family since before she was born.

Her phone rang. It was Rue Maxwell. "Hi there, Rue. How are you?"

"Jan," the woman's friendly voice said, "sorry to bother you on a Sunday night, but I've got an exciting opportunity for you and Elaine."

Rue didn't give her time to answer. "Remember the Tates, the couple you asked about on Saturday?"

The thirtysomethings from the city. "Yes, I remember them."

"Well, they're actually not just here on vacation. Lila's a freelance writer working on a piece for some small magazine. Can't remember which one or anything about it except that it has to do with food and quaint lakeside places. Long story short, she'd like to feature Tea for Two and is hoping to talk with you sometime. Can you believe it? That could be so good for business!"

"Well, yeah." As the idea took hold, Jan did feel excited about it. What a great way to get the word out about the tearoom! "Yes, I'd definitely love to talk with her. Elaine's not around right now, but I know she'd agree. Please feel free to give Lila my number."

"Actually, she's wondering if she could spend a few hours shadowing you and Elaine. You know, sort of a day in the life at the tearoom? Is there any chance that might work this week? She doesn't want to be pushy, and she promises to stay out of your way. She just fell in love with your place."

Jan didn't want to commit without at least running the idea past her cousin. "Why don't you tell her we'll sit down for tea with her tomorrow afternoon and go from there? That way Elaine and I can both talk with her."

Rue agreed to pass along the invitation to Lila.

After ending the conversation, Jan stared at the TV but didn't feel like watching anything or even reading. Feeling contented, she closed her eyes and replayed the day.

It had been fun. It was good to see Bob at church. Calling him Bobby, as she had during their growing-up years in Lancaster, had been a hard habit to break for a few weeks after they reconnected when Jan moved back to town. But he was Bob now. He was outgoing, like Peter had been, and that suited her quieter nature. And his chocolate-brown eyes weren't hard to look at. She pressed the throw pillow against the flutter in her stomach, feeling like a schoolgirl...and surprising herself by not really minding.

CHAPTER FIVE

O n Monday morning, Elaine and Jan got in Elaine's new red Chevy Malibu, equipped with fresh homemade granola bars and steaming stainless steel travel mugs, and the enticing aroma of tea filled the car. It was only seven o'clock, and most vacationers were slumbering away in cabins and B and B's, except for a few early-morning fisherman. The air was still, but Elaine knew sailboats would be skimming through the waves by noon. Both she and Jan wore colorful capri pants, cotton tops, and sandals for their morning trip out to the lakeside home of Rose and her father to look at some of Aliza Young's possessions.

As they drove along, Elaine and Jan began to brainstorm about Rose and her mysterious death certificate. "I was thinking about the fact that Rose is adopted," Jan said. "Lawyers handle adoptions, don't they?"

"I assume so," Elaine said, although since she had never been personally involved in an adoption she didn't know the process exactly.

"Well, Bob's a lawyer," Jan said. "Maybe he can help locate the attorney who handled Rose's adoption. I don't think that area of law is his specialty, but he might know where to point me. It might help Rose to know something about her mom and their circumstances before they became Youngs."

"Good idea," Elaine said.

"I'll call him when we get back home this morning." Jan took a slow sip of her tea.

Elaine couldn't help smiling at how excited her cousin seemed to be just to talk to Bob. Jan gave her a sheepish grin and then continued. "Did you learn anything from Nathan? You were on the phone for a while last night."

"I know. I wasn't expecting to talk so long, but we got to rehashing old times, and I didn't notice the clock. He told me about his wife, Julia, and how she left him almost a decade ago."

"Oh, I'm so sorry to hear that," Jan said.

"I was sorry too, although Nathan said that after they divorced they were able to be amicable with one another. It was difficult for them after their kids grew up—they realized that they hadn't put in the work to grow together while they were raising their family and instead had grown apart. Sadly, the gap between them was more than they could overcome, even though they tried counseling."

Nathan had told Elaine, *"The divorce made me realize I need to take time every now and then to reflect on who I am and who I'm becoming. I know myself much better now."* Elaine agreed completely. She knew herself—and frankly, liked herself—much better now, in her midfifties, than she ever had when she was younger. "Anyway, Nathan said he'll call a document expert, Neal Danielson, this morning. He's hoping to bring him to the tearoom later today to look at the death certificate."

Crossing her ankles in the passenger seat, Jan swallowed her last bite of her granola bar. "I'm dying to know what he'll have to say about it." She watched the scenery swishing by outside the passenger window for a moment and then glanced ahead. "I think the Youngs' place should be coming up soon."

"Still a couple more miles, according to Rose's directions." Elaine steered around a bend. "Nathan said Neal's been in the business for nearly thirty years, and he's seen some amazing documents. A lot of old family letters found in attics, old drafts of wills that surviving relatives fight over, that kind of thing."

"I wonder if this will be his first death certificate for a living person," Jan mused.

Elaine chuckled. "I'd guess those don't show up very often. Anyhow, Nathan will text me when he has a time set to come by."

"Great. And I'll call Bob later, after he has a chance to get settled into his work week." Jan pointed out a doe with two spotted fawns at the edge of a stretch of evergreens. The mama looked up as the Malibu rumbled near, while her babies ambled close by. "Seeing deer around here never gets old."

"Nope. I'm so glad this area hasn't gotten too built up to run them off." Elaine glanced over at her cousin. "So tell me more about this article about Tea for Two."

"Rue called and said one of her guests wants to feature us in a magazine. The writer wants to spend a few hours in the tearoom, 'shadowing us,' she called it, and I suggested she come in for tea this afternoon to give us the details."

"That sounds interesting. And that's fine, if you think we can fit in one more thing today."

"We do have a lot going on, but it could be worth the publicity we could get." Jan gestured ahead. "I think that's the two-mile sign to Penzance coming up."

As they passed the sign, Elaine slowed the car around another bend, and the wooded area opened into a clearing and a driveway on the left. A blue Cape Cod house stood back off the road, its three second-story dormer windows welcoming visitors like wide-open eyes.

"*Ooh*, what a pretty house." Jan sat forward. "I like the brick steps to the covered porch."

"It is charming," Elaine agreed. "I'm glad for the chance to see where Rose lives. Helps me feel I know her a little better. And maybe we can learn more about her mother too."

White peony bushes bloomed on both sides of the three steps up to the porch and the double wooden front doors. Urns with small pines graced either side of the door frame.

About fifty yards from the road, the driveway split. One stretch continued to the right, toward the attached garage of the home. The other veered left to a detached two-story garage that matched the house. A yellow Beetle was parked in front of that outbuilding, and a petite woman with short brown hair, who appeared to be in her early twenties, was coming down the outside staircase that led from the second level. Beyond the house, the lake shimmered and a fish jumped by the dock, where a classic-looking red motorboat sat on a lift above the water.

"That must be their tenant." Elaine pulled into a space out of the Beetle's way between the house and detached garage and shut off the engine. Both cousins gathered their purses and mugs and were shutting their doors when soft footsteps sounded on the concrete. Elaine turned to see the young woman approach with a big smile and her hand outstretched. She was tanned and toned like a gymnast and wore a purple tank top, white cutoff shorts, and purple Chuck Taylor canvas shoes. Long gold earrings dangled to her collarbone.

"Hi! I'm Allie McCall."

Elaine shook her hand as Jan rounded the car to stand beside her.

Allie held out a hand to Jan. "Are you here to see Clifton? He already left this morning, but Rose is still home. I live above their garage." She rummaged in her bulky purple shoulder bag and held out a business card. "I'm new in town. I'm a stylist at A Cut Above in Penzance, if you're ever looking for something new." She brushed her hair back over her ear and made her dangling earrings catch the light as they swayed.

Elaine took the card and thanked her, and Jan took a step toward the house.

But Allie hadn't finished. "Or maybe you're visiting Rose, not Clifton? She's working for two older women now." Allie's long eyelashes batted a couple of times.

Jan opened her mouth but then shut it and cast a mischievous grin Elaine's way.

"It was nice to meet you, Allie," Elaine replied efficiently. "But we better go so we don't keep Rose waiting…Jan?"

"Right. You have a good day, Allie. It was nice to meet you."

The cousins began the trek to the door as Allie's voice carried after them. "Sure thing."

Waving over their heads as they walked away, Elaine and Jan followed the brick path from the driveway to the porch steps, which they jogged up side by side. As Jan rapped the door knocker, she rolled her eyes. "Older, my foot."

Elaine stifled a laugh as the door swung open.

Rose stood inside and motioned them into the light-filled entry. Dressed in a lime-green cotton shift dress, with her hair twisted up in a clip, Rose had more color in her face and looked more rested this morning than the day before. She motioned them into the light-filled entry with a welcoming smile. "Hey there. Come on in."

They hugged their greetings, and Rose offered them something to drink. Elaine held up her mug. "Still working on my tea, but I'd love to see your home. It looks lovely."

"I'll give you the nickel tour. Why don't you put your bags down first?" She pointed to a hall tree by the door that had been converted from an antique church pew. Several baskets with shoes sat beneath it. The cousins deposited their purses and followed Rose through the main floor of the home to the living room and sitting room. The living room had white trim, light walls, and a TV and brown leather sectional; the sitting room had stained wood trim, a fireplace and rustic mantel, and over-stuffed chairs. Dozens of books and photo albums were tucked on to an entire wall of built-in shelves, Elaine noted with some envy.

"Mom wasn't much of a TV watcher, but she loved to read. She could finish a book a day if she had time."

"A kindred spirit," Elaine replied. A quick perusal told her that the shelves were organized by genre and were loaded with both fiction and nonfiction, classics as well as newer releases, biographies, and a shelf full of European history books, mainly German. And seven or eight thick photo albums.

Bookends and knickknacks separated the sections and provided breaks in the rows of spines. Elaine spotted a couple of crosses, several glass figurines, and a number of picture frames with photos of Aliza, Rose, and Clifton through the years. Jan had stepped closer and seemed taken by the glimpses before her of the family's life.

A porcelain doll on the end of one shelf caught Elaine's eye. She sat with her legs hanging over the edge. Her blonde curls were slightly rumpled, but her cheeks still glowed pink, and her blue eyes were wide open and smiling. She wore a pink satin dress, white pinafore, and glossy painted black Mary Janes.

Before Elaine could open her mouth to comment, Jan pointed. "What a beautiful doll! Was that your mother's?"

"Actually, she was mine...although I wasn't really allowed to play with her." Rose added the last part as an afterthought, then shrugged. "Mom said some toys were for playing and others were for looking at. Beatrice was a shelf doll."

Elaine grinned. "I remember a few dolls that my daughter, Sasha, wore out with love."

Next, Rose showed them the dining room with its polished Queen Anne table and china cabinet and the quaint kitchen with Corian countertops and cherry cabinets, before leading them up the open staircase.

"All the bedrooms are up here," she said at the top. Past a bathroom and at the far end of the landing, she stopped. "This guest room has a door in the closet that leads up to attic space over the garage." Inside the room, she flipped on a light switch by the large walk-in closet and led them up four steps at the back of it.

At the top, the dimly lit space opened into a drywalled room about ten feet by twelve feet. A window looked out over the lake and let in enough morning light for the three to see dust motes floating in the air beneath the weathered wood rafters.

Stacked boxes, plastic bins, trays of Christmas décor, and an old iron headboard left very little open floor space.

Rose rubbed her forehead before picking her way to the corner at the right of the window. The cousins stood with her in front of the iron headboard.

"This is where I found the certificate. Here, under the foot of this headboard, tucked back near that box behind it." Rose tugged one end of the headboard. "If you wouldn't mind helping me move this thing, we can get to the box. I think the certificate may have been inside it at some point."

Together the three women shuffled the heavy headboard across the room and propped it against some sturdy-looking bins, then turned back to the dusty, unmarked box. Rose reached over and pulled a folded pillowcase from a nearby bin marked Old Linens and wiped it off.

With a look of determination on her face, Rose leaned down and broke the packing tape, then gingerly lifted back the flaps. A white lace cloth lay across the top.

Rose gasped. "Mom's tablecloth," she whispered. "I haven't seen this in years." She pulled the fabric completely out of the box and let it unfold. Yards of beautifully crafted lace cascaded to the floor and hung like a waterfall from her fingertips. Tears filled her eyes and fell on the section she held to her cheeks, but she was glowing.

Elaine and Jan reached out to feel its texture.

"Mom made this tablecloth before I was born, and she kept it on the dining room table for years. I had no idea it's been up here; I was probably away at college when she put it away."

Elaine noticed Jan, a skilled seamstress, studying it. Jan's eyes held wonder as she spoke. "Rose, this is gorgeous. Your mother made this?"

"*Mm-hmm.* One thing she did tell me was that she learned lace-making from her mother. She tried to teach me a few things when I was thirteen or fourteen, but I wasn't interested back then. I thought it seemed old-fashioned."

Elaine chuckled. "*Old* is in the eye of the beholder, it seems."

"Ugh." Jan looked exasperated, and Rose looked questioningly at them.

"We were called old this morning when we arrived," Elaine explained. "Well, *older* anyway."

Rose groaned. "You met Allie."

Jan laughed.

"I'm sorry about that. Allie's okay, but she can be a little clueless sometimes. She doesn't always think before she speaks. You two are hardly *old.*"

"I suppose it's a matter of perspective," Jan said. She looked as if she was holding back a laugh.

Rose looked like she was trying to contain a smile. "My dad says she just doesn't have all the dumb out of her yet, but life will fix that soon enough."

The three of them shared a hearty laugh.

"She's always in a good mood," Rose said, "but sometimes she does act like a busybody. I actually found her in the house last week."

"Uninvited?" Elaine dropped her smile and raised her eyebrows.

"Yep. I came in from work one evening, and she was in the sitting room, looking at our photo albums. Dad and I haven't made a big deal of locking the front door, even though Mom was always strict about it. But since last week I've locked it every day."

"Did you ask her what she was doing?" Jan asked.

Rose nodded. "She wondered what it looked like inside. And she wanted to borrow some sugar."

"Sugar." Elaine could tell Rose hadn't bought that excuse either.

"I'm sure she didn't mean harm. She's just nosy, I think. Other than that, she's been a good renter."

"She'll grow up sometime, I suppose." Jan shrugged. "I'd love to look at this tablecloth more closely. I do some needlepoint but haven't ever tried making lace."

"You're welcome to take it for a few days," Rose offered, handing the heirloom to Jan.

Jan refolded it while Rose took another stack of lace fabric from the box. Near giddiness seemed to take over Rose as she held up one after another smaller items, including several handkerchiefs and two intricate ornaments.

She passed each one to Jan and then Elaine. "See the pictures in them? Mom said her family used to sew animals, flowers, crosses, trees, names into the lace...anything that added uniqueness. It was sort of her family's signature."

Sure enough, the handkerchief Elaine held had a picture of two doves in the corner.

"Oh, look!" Jan exclaimed. "There's a mountain with the sun over it." She held up an ornament for the others to see.

Minutes passed while they studied the lace, and then Rose turned back to the box. Without a word, she pulled out a brown leather scrapbook. She seemed to consider opening it but then handed it to Elaine and reached into the box one more time to remove a white envelope that had seen better days, with addresses written in German. "That's the last of it."

They moved closer to the light from the window and sat in a huddle on the floor. Elaine lifted back the cover of the scrapbook. Pressed flat on the top page were a couple of folded newspaper stories with dry, yellowed edges that showed their age. Elaine picked up the first one, unfolded it carefully, and smoothed the darkened creases. An article filled the page, along with a black-and-white photo of a handsome elderly couple in evening wear. The woman's hair was light and cut in a manicured short style. The man had a light-colored mustache. Both had a proud lift to their chins.

Her curiosity piqued, Elaine focused on the text, only to find, to her disappointment, that the article was written in German. She had picked up a few phrases of the language during her international life as a military wife, but not enough to guess at the headline's translation—

"*Stasi Officer and Wife Die in Car Accident,*" Rose read out loud.

Elaine looked up at her. "You know German."

"Sure, some. My mother's influence. And some of my own casual study." She didn't look away from the article.

It was dated March 17, 2005. Elaine did a double take. "Look at the caption."

Rose's hand flew to her mouth.

"Georg and Berta *Schultz*," Jan said. "The last name on the death certificate!"

CHAPTER SIX

E laine held up the article so they all could see it better.

Rose's clear blue eyes moved back and forth as she scanned. "I can read enough to understand that Georg was a high-ranking official in the *Stasi*." She pronounced the word "SHTA-zee." "Weren't they sort of like the police?"

"Yes, the secret police of *East* Germany." Elaine had thought Rose's German roots were West German.

Jan pointed to the date. "March 2005. That was more than a decade after the Berlin Wall fell. If I remember correctly, the wall came down in November 1989."

"So whoever Georg and Berta Schultz were," Elaine spoke slowly, "they lived on the Communist side. What used to be East Berlin."

Rose looked crestfallen. "They were part of that government." Her voice sounded empty.

Elaine knew Rose was sure the article connected her past with that heritage, one of restricted freedom, corrupt leadership, hardship, and harsh penalties for anyone who didn't abide by the government's demands. "We still don't know who they were, Rose. We can't make any assumptions about that just yet." But looking into the faces of the man and woman, she admitted to herself that they didn't contain much warmth.

"Let's see the other article," Jan suggested.

Elaine unfolded the second paper and smoothed the creases that cut through the text and the accompanying photo of the crumbling Berlin Wall. Throngs of people with mallets and picks appeared to be hacking away at the country's thirty-year symbol of Cold War imprisonment. The article was from the *Morning Sentinel* and was dated November 9, 1999, a tenth-anniversary story of the Wall's demise.

Elaine remembered that historic week nearly twenty-seven years earlier. "Ben was stationed in West Germany back then," she offered. Jared had been about three at the time; Sasha hadn't yet been born. Elaine had been juggling life with a pre-schooler and keeping things running at home with only a few short years of experience living abroad and no relatives near for support. It had been a stressful time, but exciting to have a front-and-center view of history in the making.

Rose reached for the articles. "I was born a few months after the wall fell. These people, whoever they were, died when I was almost fifteen."

Elaine recalled Rose's story of finding her childhood necklace when she was about fifteen years old, and Aliza's shocked reaction. And Rose's memory of her mother making excuses about hiding a piece of paper behind her back. A Christmas list, really? Or possibly an article about the deaths of a Stasi couple? The similar time frame between those memories and the 2005 article seemed coincidental.

Jan glanced at her watch. "We do need to keep an eye on the time," she reminded Elaine. "Should we see what else is in the album?"

The first page held a faded color picture of two young women who appeared to be in their early twenties. They were standing near a fence with a white warehouse-type building in the background. Both had shoulder-length hair and wore pants and jackets and simple jewelry.

A second picture showed the same scene but closer up. A breeze must have blown through because both women had a hand raised to hold their hair back from their faces. That photo captured more detail of their features and even the shine on the bracelet hanging on the raised forearm of the woman on the left.

Rose pointed to the woman on the right. "That's Mom."

Elaine and Jan leaned in. "She was lovely," Elaine said, smiling.

"*Mm-hmm.* And she hardly ever wore makeup."

"You inherited that from her, Rose. Natural beauty," Jan said. "Do you recognize her friend? She's very pretty too."

Elaine thought the other woman looked taller, although it was hard to be sure since she was leaning against the fence in the first picture. Aliza was standing more upright.

"I've never seen her. I don't recognize that building either."

Jan pulled the picture closer. "Can you make out the sign on it?"

Leave it to detail-oriented Jan to notice the little things. Sure enough, on the more distant picture, in text that was somewhat out of focus, a placard declared something about the building. Only a blurred corner of it appeared in the close-up picture.

"I think it says 'Plau'... 'Plauener'?" Jan squinted.

Rose peered at it intently. "PLOW-en-er," she said. "I think Plauen is a town name in Germany."

"Hang on." Elaine got up and hurried from the room. She retrieved her phone from her purse and returned to the attic with it a few seconds later. "Google should tell us what that means." She typed in *Plauen* and clicked her tongue at the links that popped up. "Plauener *Spitze*, Plauen Lace, *Spitzen*, die *Spitze*, lace..."

"Of course," Rose said. "*Spitze*. Lace. So *Plauener Spitze* means lace from Plauen. Maybe that building was a school, and her friend was a classmate." She squinted at the photo. "She looks very young."

"Could be," Jan mused. "Or maybe they were teachers there."

"It could be a factory where they worked." Elaine touched one of the links and summarized its contents for Jan and Rose. "Looks like Plauen lace and embroidery is a centuries-old specialty originally from the city of Plauen, Germany. *Hmm*. There's a lot more here, for later. Your mom kept these things together—the Stasi couple, the Berlin Wall, the lace factory, and the lace—for a reason, I'd guess. They've got to be connected."

The next couple of pages showed scenic photographs of mountains and a couple of large stone homes, but nothing that revealed anything personal about Aliza. The rest of the pages were empty, but as Elaine flipped through them, the envelope they'd forgotten about dropped to the floor.

Rose picked it up. It had been opened, so she pulled out the three folded pages and smoothed them out. The writing was in a masculine script, though somewhat shaky, and was dated February 1975. It was addressed to *Mein Schatzi*.

"My darling or my little treasure," Rose translated. A cloud scooted past the sun and dimmed the light from the window as a hush fell across the attic while Rose read silently. Every now and then her mouth puckered as she appeared to stumble over difficulty with a translation or perhaps interpreting the writer's penmanship.

Elaine gave Jan a questioning look and gently pulled the empty envelope from beneath Rose's hand. She checked the postmark date and location, then handed it to Jan. The return address showed the letter was from a man named Ernst Beck at Keibelstrasse prison in East Berlin.

Finally after a few minutes, Rose cleared her throat and shifted position. "This letter is from a father in prison to his daughter, Fredda. She turned nine shortly after he sent it to her. He wrote how sad he was to miss her birthday. He believed she would be even more beautiful at nine than the last time he saw her two years earlier, when he was arrested."

"Does it say what he was in prison for?" Jan asked.

"Well, he mentioned something about a friend there, another political prisoner—so he wasn't entirely lonesome, he wrote. It's a beautiful letter."

Rose looked up. "I wonder if Fredda was my mom's friend in that picture." She turned the scrapbook pages back to the beginning and traced a finger along her mother's likeness.

Elaine had been thinking something along those lines, but not quite the same as Rose. She wasn't ready to voice her idea though. "Did he say anything else?"

"Just to take care of her mother. He sounds very loving and affectionate. He doesn't sound like a hardened criminal." She smiled at the cousins. "My mom sometimes called me *mein Schatzi*."

Elaine kept quiet, but her suspicions grew.

"He may not have been a criminal at all," Jan offered. "Not really, anyway."

Elaine thought about it. "That's true. When we were in West Germany, we'd hear stories about the East German government punishing people just for disagreeing with their laws or even expressing their opinions about the government. It was one way they kept order, or at least fear, in the people. They'd throw them in prison for minor things."

"I remember Amy studying all of that for a school project," Jan said. "She couldn't get over the fact that innocent people were treated like traitors."

Rose folded the letter and took the envelope from Elaine, pausing to stare at the addresses. "Ernst Beck. So his daughter was Fredda Beck. She lived in East Germany too, but not Berlin."

Elaine pinched the bridge of her nose. She had to ask. "Rose, how old was your mother when she passed away?"

"Fifty. Why?"

Elaine had already done the calculations. "So she was born in 1966, right?"

"Yes. March 4, 1966."

A barely noticeable lift of Jan's chin let Elaine know that her cousin was catching on. And Rose held Elaine's gaze without flinching, her eyes widening slightly, which told Elaine that Rose understood too. "She would've been nine a month after this letter was postmarked."

Rose swallowed slowly. "You're saying my mother may have been one and the same as Fredda Beck."

"It seems like a possibility," Elaine answered gently.

Rose laced her fingers over the letter and held it to her chest. "I think it might be time to talk to Dad again tonight."

From either side, Jan and Elaine laid reassuring hands over hers.

"That makes sense to me. He may be able to help sort through this," Jan said, "no matter what he does or doesn't know."

Rose stood, still holding the envelope. She checked her watch while the cousins stood next to her. "We need to get to work," she said, as the cloud moved by and the sun shone brightly through the window once more.

As they gathered their purses to leave, Jan mentioned her idea to ask Bob's help in locating the Young family's adoption lawyer. "Do you happen to have a copy of your adoptive birth certificate? My friend is a lawyer and he may be able to help us figure out more about your adoption."

Rose agreed and went to get it. While she was gone, Jan motioned Elaine into the sitting room. "When Rose showed us this room, I noticed some of the titles, and I think they could help us find out more about those things in the box."

Jan pointed to the shelf full of European books, and each of them pulled down several references on lace-making, the history of lace, Stasi prisons and the East German government, and the Berlin Wall.

"These ought to make for interesting reading," Elaine said, carrying a load of books back to the entry as Rose returned. Rose handed Elaine her birth certificate. Elaine studied it for a moment, finding the information she needed. According to the certificate, Rose had been born in a hospital in Augusta.

"Rose, could we borrow these books?" Jan asked, gesturing toward the stack. "I have a feeling they might shed a little light on your mom and her life."

"Sure, if you think it could help." Rose reached for the top book on Elaine's pile, saying she never understood why her mother was reading about German prisons. She leafed through the bulky book, and as she did, a piece of parchment drifted back to the floor. All three of the women looked down simultaneously.

Elaine set her stack on the entry pew and picked up the paper. She couldn't believe what she was seeing. It was a death certificate for Fredda Beck, dated November 17, 1991, the same date as Tatiana Rose's.

CHAPTER SEVEN

It was nine thirty as Jan, Elaine, and Rose left Rose's driveway in two cars, heading toward the tearoom, and Jan knew the next few hours would be busy. The books from the Youngs' shelves and the folded lace tablecloth sat on the backseat of Elaine's car, and Rose's birth certificate was nestled securely away in Jan's purse. They had left the smaller lace items in the attic box.

As Elaine drove, Jan called Bob. She explained briefly that she needed some legal advice for a friend, and could she hire him for an hour or so to pick his brain about an adoption that happened almost twenty-five years ago? She reached for her lipstick in her purse and applied it while he answered.

"Of course I'll help you, Jan, but only if you don't say anything more about payment."

His smile was almost audible, and she returned it into the phone. "Thanks, Bob."

"In fact, if you're free tomorrow after work, why don't I pick you up and we can talk about it over supper? Have you been to the Hearthside yet? They serve a great prime rib. And their lobster bisque? It's the best!"

She liked the thought of an evening out with Bob, but she wasn't going to assume he meant anything more than a meal between friends. Still, they were friends by now, right? She felt sure enough to call it that. "It would be nice to eat someone else's cooking for a change." She gave Elaine an apologetic smile.

"Super. I'll make reservations and swing by around seven. See you soon, Jan."

She put her phone back in her purse and rubbed her lips together one more time to smooth her lipstick, then returned the conversation to their discoveries at the Young house. "Any ideas where we go from here?" Elaine was good at knowing what to look into next.

Elaine turned on the windshield washer. "Let's think this through while it's still fresh."

The wiper blades swish-swished the streams of liquid until the view was clear again while Jan rummaged in her purse for a pen and scrap paper to jot notes. "We found pieces of lace, which fit with what Aliza told Rose about her family lace-making." She wrote *lace pieces/tablecloth*. "I borrowed a book about the art of lace-making from their shelves. I'll look through it tonight. I'm hoping it'll at least help me understand how the art was passed down in families, and maybe even mention specific family businesses."

"And I found a book about the history of lace in Europe. Who knows? Maybe it'll have some information about factories or schools in Germany."

"Sounds good. We don't know why Aliza and her friend, whoever she was, were standing in front of a building that must be in Plauen, a town known for its lace-making." Jan wrote *Who is friend? Plauen building—school/factory?*

"And what about the photo of the Schultzes?" Elaine asked next, and Jan wrote down their names. "What was their relationship to Tatiana Rose Schultz? There's also Ernst Beck's letter to Fredda Beck. Was there a connection between Ernst Beck and that Stasi official, Georg Schultz, and his wife, Berta?"

"Do you think Aliza could've been reminded of that part of her past the weekend Clifton and Rose were away when Rose was fifteen?" Jan asked.

"Possibly. What if she saw the article about their deaths, and it prompted her to pull out some old heirlooms, like Tatiana's necklace?"

Elaine nodded in agreement. "If Aliza was Fredda, and if there is a connection between Ernst and the Schultzes, then the Schultz connection would also connect Rose to them—and that could start to explain the Schultz name on a fake death certificate for Rose…But let's keep thinking through this. I can look into Keibelstrasse prison and see if I can find out why Ernst Beck was there. And when. Maybe it'll tell something of his background."

"Good." Jan jotted down their ideas. She felt reenergized by her conversation with Bob and practical tasks to be done, though privately she wondered how many records might still exist from an East German prison. Still, with the Internet providing unprecedented access to such things, who knew until they started looking?

"I'll look into the Augusta hospital about this birth certificate of Rose's and see if they keep records that far back. It wouldn't hurt to make sure she really was born there. Depending on how Bob can help, I hope to find out whether the hospital listed on this birth certificate for Rose Tatiana Young matches her original one when she was born there as Rose Tatiana Sims."

"We ought to look into Hans Sims too. He was German, like Aliza. Maybe *he* has relatives who can help put the pieces together." Elaine pulled into the garage and shut off the engine.

"What I'd give for one good conversation with Rose's mother," Jan said. "Makes me wish we'd moved back here a few months earlier so we could've gotten to know her better."

Jan remembered the day they'd met Aliza. It was the one time she came in to see Rose at the tearoom. The meeting had been brief, but Aliza was quietly friendly and obviously loved and was fiercely proud of her daughter.

"One conversation about who she was," Jan went on, "and a lesson in lacework. Can you believe how talented she was? Her work is beautiful. I can't imagine why she'd pack away that tablecloth instead of displaying it."

"Me neither. And who knows how any of those details fit with the death certificates. Nathan and I texted as we were leaving Rose's. He and Neal, the document expert, are coming over at lunchtime to look at them."

By the time they had arrived home and parked Elaine's Malibu, there were only minutes to spare before the tearoom opened. They quickly tucked the tablecloth and the books behind the counter until they had time to look at them again, and they scurried about, their division of labor now a familiar, comfortable routine as they prepared the tearoom for their guests. Jan and Rose helped Elaine set up an easel with a sign on it near the front to announce the food drive that would last through the holiday the following week.

"Oh no." Elaine grimaced as Jan adjusted the sign. "I completely forgot to deliver my food-drive flyers to the other businesses to put on their counters."

Rose was setting out napkins on tables in the east parlor. "Why don't I drop them off? I could be back in thirty minutes."

Elaine thanked her and told her where the flyers were in the office. "Most of the other businesses on Main Street agreed to set them out, so that includes Sylvia's Closet, A Little Something, and Kate's Diner to the east. Then the Bookworm, the Pine Tree Grill, the marina bait shop, the art gallery and What-Not to the west. And across the street from us, you can drop off a bunch at Sugar Plum, Oldies But Goodies, Gift Me., and the general store. When I offered to head up the food drive, I hoped to bring the town to Tea for Two when they drop off their donations. I don't suppose it's wrong to have an ulterior motive, is it? Give back to the community and hope they'll keep us in business?"

"It's a great idea, Elaine." Rose smiled as she gathered her purse and left to deliver the flyers.

"Can't fault her for lack of pluck, that's for sure," Jan said as she headed back to the kitchen. She wanted to be sure the teas she had started were steeping well. Raising her voice as she walked away, she added, "I'll have some fresh boxed dozens ready for the display case in a few minutes. It's maple mini croissants, raspberry thumbprints, almond tassies, plum tarts, German chocolate brownies, lemon poppyseed muffins, and

Amish sugar cookies." She glanced back at her cousin. "And please pray I don't do some stress eating while I'm back there!"

*J*AN SEEMS TO *have a unique bounce in her step today,* Elaine thought as she rearranged the parlor chairs and tables in preparation for opening. She was happy for the relationship that was obviously developing between Jan and Bob, even though she wasn't sure how much Jan was admitting to herself yet. The idea of new romance didn't appeal to Elaine's own heart yet, but months ago she'd decided to trust that God's new plans for her would come in His timing. She was going to stick to that and be happy today.

Just before ten o'clock Elaine unlocked the front door and stepped outside to sweep the front porch and steps. There. Now they were ready for business. She waved to Sylvia Flood next door, who was opening her vintage clothing store. Elaine looked east and west down Main Street. A pair of bicyclists weaved on the sidewalk and a few vehicles cruised along. Several parking spaces were already taken in front of stores. The business section of Lancaster was alive and well that Monday morning. She saw Rose's CRV pull into a space in front of the Pine Tree Grill two doors down to the west. Rose hopped out of her car with a stack of flyers and jogged into the restaurant.

The morning sped by after Rose returned as customers stopped in between shopping errands. Dutch Bigelow, a retired state police detective, was the first to drop off donations. He came in with several loaded plastic grocery bags. "I saw your brochures when I took my carvings to Gift Me," he said.

"I've seen your work there!" Elaine said. "It's so beautiful!" She'd seen several pieces she thought might make wonderful gifts.

Dutch ducked his head modestly in acknowledgment and smiled. "I appreciate that. I guess I don't think of it as 'work,' because I enjoy it so much."

Elaine smiled. "It's never really work when you love doing it."

He held up the bags he had brought in with him. "Where can I put these?"

"Follow me." Leaving Rose to handle the counter and the customers in both parlors, Elaine led Dutch back to the dining room to leave the bags, and then she seated him in the east parlor and took his order of green tea and a lemon poppyseed muffin.

Three more townspeople dropped off canned and dried goods in the first hour, and Elaine was excited about the pile that had already filled up half of the dining room table.

Around eleven o'clock, two men came in the door, the second one carrying a brown leather attaché. She recognized the first man as J. Eisley Segouri. Tall and bone-thin with jet-black hair, he filled the room with a boisterous hello to everyone. "Fine place you've got here, Ms....?"

She wished she'd taken longer ringing up the previous customers, but she smiled pleasantly. "Cook. Elaine Cook. Welcome to Tea for Two."

Elaine took two menus and saw a table near Diane Blanchett, owner of Computer Gal, who was chatting over steaming drinks with a friend. Elaine smiled at the two women as if she'd never felt a stressful moment in her life, then got Segouri's attention.

"Right this way." She led him to the west parlor where she could keep an eye on him from the counter and where he wasn't center stage. "This is perfect." She placed the menus on the table. "Enjoy some tea and Jan's delicious desserts."

"Thank you. My name is J. Eisley Segouri, and I would like your vote"—he gestured to his unnamed right-hand man, who started to pull a campaign postcard from his attaché—"in the election." He flashed a big salesman grin. "We've only two weeks to go, dear."

Elaine glanced back toward the counter, where Jan watched the interaction as she handed change to a customer. Elaine politely took the postcard and motioned Segouri's right-hand man to another seat at the table.

Segouri said, "This is my campaign manager, Charles Shaver. As I was saying, I've got the experience our great little town of Lancaster needs to bring it up to par—"

"Pleased to meet you, Mr. Shaver," Elaine interrupted. "Enjoy our selections from the menu."

She straightened but cringed when she realized she'd seated the two men next to the table where Macy Atherton and her daughter-in-law, Zale, were no longer paying attention to their raspberry thumbprints. Instead, Macy was staring tight-lipped at Segouri, and Zale was staring nervously at her mother-in-law.

The next instant, Rose appeared at the women's table with a simple pine-green teapot. "Macy, Zale, how are you this morning? Let me refresh your tea." Macy owned Green Glade cottages. She was a regular customer at Tea for Two, and even though she found fault with something nearly every time she came in, she continued to come back and often recommended the tearoom to her guests.

Macy turned her disapproving expression on Rose, and Elaine could have hugged Rose. She had placed herself in the line of Macy's fire by distracting the woman from J. Eisley's scene.

Macy harrumphed but turned back to her own table. "These cookies are tasteless."

"I'll be happy to bring you a couple of croissants instead. You always seem to like those." Rose reached for the plate in front of Macy.

"No, no," Macy grumped. "These'll do. I need to get back to work."

"They're very good, Rose," Zale commented quietly, earning a patronizing look from her mother-in-law.

J. Eisley, Charles, and Elaine had been sidetracked by the exchange at Macy's table, but to Elaine's chagrin, J. Eisley stood and leaned over with his hand outstretched to Zale.

"I don't believe we've met," he said to her. "I am J. Eisley Seg—"

"We know who you are, Mr. Eisley," Macy interrupted.

"It's J. Seguor— I mean Eisley. It's J. Eisley. And whom do I have the pleasure of meeting?" J. Eisley released Zale's hand and extended his own to Macy.

"I'm Macy Atherton, and I'll be voting for Clifton Young." Her words were clipped and biting.

The temperature rose as all eyes in the west parlor turned toward the debate that was steeping in front of Elaine.

CHAPTER EIGHT

Jan eyed the customers who were watching the mounting tension in the west parlor. Fortunately, those in the east parlor with a view of the scene seemed oblivious so far.

When Elaine squared her shoulders, Jan knew she was about to nip the situation in the bud.

"Mr. Segouri, let's save the campaigning for outside." Elaine kept her voice low but authoritative. "Macy, I'm sure you understand. You can talk about all this at the debate Thursday night." For a second time she took J. Eisley's arm and helped him to his seat.

"Let's go, Zale." Macy stood and pulled her shoulder bag from the back of her chair.

Jan was glad to see Macy relent. A couple of minutes later, Jan finished ringing her up, handed her the box of scones Macy bought to go, and watched the door close behind the cantankerous woman and her long-suffering daughter-in-law.

The parlors and porch tables emptied as the lunch hour approached. Some days a few customers lingered through the noon hour, but Jan was grateful for the momentary emptiness. Perhaps the breather would stretch for a while longer.

Promptly at noon, Nathan's familiar voice carried from the front of the house while she and Rose were in the kitchen plating tuna sandwiches and fruit salad for the meeting.

Pushing the food cart, they joined the others in the quiet front half of the house. Jan looked through the windows to the side porch and was glad that the only two occupied tables were out there, leaving the parlors private.

Nathan introduced Neal Danielson, the documents expert from Augusta. Jan couldn't help noticing the man's vivid red hair as she greeted him. "Would you like to sit here?" Jan suggested, gesturing to a table near the front of the room. From that position in the east parlor, she could keep an eye on the rest of the tables so that Elaine and Rose could stay in the meeting.

Neal was talkative about his work while they ate. Halfway through Jan's brownies and sugar cookies, Rose slid the two death certificates across the table to him. "I don't know how much Elaine might have told you, but I think these may be for me and...possibly my mother, who passed away—in truth— last month."

"I'm sorry to hear about your mother," Neal said sincerely as he slipped a pair of reading glasses from his shirt pocket and settled them on the bridge of his nose. Loupes stuck out about a half inch off the fronts of both lenses. For several minutes he looked at the documents, his mouth twitching occasionally as he studied them.

He set the parchments side by side on the table and with his finger traced the outline of the circular, faded ink stamp on each one. He leaned closer, gazed through the loupes, picked up the document with Fredda's name, and held it to the window's light.

The air conditioner kicked on quietly and Jan snuck a look at her watch. It was almost twelve thirty. Early-afternoon customers could arrive anytime. She surveyed the parlor. Right now the fireplace's wood box seemed like a big mouth gaping at the reason for this meeting.

Neal set the certificate back on the table and took a three-ring binder from his briefcase. He flipped through a number of pages containing photocopies of documents and compared the ones Rose had given him with those.

Finally, he looked at Rose over the rims of his glasses. "They could be authentic. These were issued from Germany a year after the two sides had been reunited. I've seen many birth and death certificates from there over the years, and while the forms change slightly, the official markings look good. The seals look official, and the paper does too.

"The date of death on both—November 17, 1991—was two years after the Wall came down. The two Germanys had been reunified by then, but certainly not everyone was happy about it. I'm always curious to see documents from that era.

"To be honest," he continued, "if these looked like false *birth* certificates and were from West Germany with a date before the Wall fell, I'd question them more because that would mean someone was trying to get *into* that country, possibly to escape the East. Death certificates don't immediately raise any special red flags."

He removed his unique glasses and set them on the table, then went on. "The region was still rife with spies at this time.

Everyone was keeping tabs on everyone else, so fake papers were not uncommon. Forgers could make a decent side income for any number of reasons."

He paused to chew a bite of cookie. "All in all, I don't see anything unusual in these documents. They could be genuine; they could be forgeries. The most notable thing about them is that they share a death date."

All of that was interesting, Jan thought, but it didn't explain the oddness of Aliza having both documents in her possession, or that a woman her age and a child with her own daughter's birthdate and similar name were on record as having died the same day.

But could the changing politics in Germany at the time have had anything to do with the death certificates? Aliza's news clippings about the Stasi official's death and the Berlin Wall, and Ernst Beck's letter...all were curious and suggested a connection. How closely did those events touch Aliza? And more to the point, what did any of it mean for Rose?

Neal put his glasses away. "I can run more tests, but I'll have to take the parchments to my lab. A couple of caveats though: Those tests wouldn't necessarily prove their genuineness. They'd only detect any falsities."

He paused as if waiting for everyone to understand his distinction. "Forgers often don't use the same mechanics or equipment as the creators of official documents. Sometimes we can find anomalies like awkward impressions, indentations, or signs of wear on the paper that indicate a document wasn't created just right. It would look rougher, basically. But let's say nothing unusual turns up—that still doesn't guarantee they're authentic. It only means we didn't find any discrepancies."

He stopped speaking until Rose met his gaze. "If these aren't authentic, they're very good forgeries, which means the forger had decent equipment. So I want you know that I am not expecting to find amateur mistakes."

He smiled gently but Rose looked deflated. "I'm happy to run the tests anyway. They'll take some time, maybe a few days." He looked again at the two documents. "And the creases in them could skew results."

The front door swung open and two icons of Lancaster, retired doctor Tyson McInnis and his wife, Claudia, entered the tearoom. Jan started to get up, but Claudia waved her back and pointed to the porch. Jan held up two fingers to indicate she'd be out to take their orders in a couple of minutes, and the elderly couple went back outside.

Elaine rested her elbows on the table and addressed Neal. "So what you're saying is you think they are real but it's worth a shot to make sure?"

When the man nodded, Elaine offered to take the certificates back to the office and make a copy of each one for Rose before handing the originals over to Neal.

When she returned, the cousins thanked Nathan for introducing them to Neal, and thanked Neal for his expert help. Elaine handed him the original certificates and gave the copies to Rose. Rose, too, thanked the men for their time and help, even though Jan thought she looked mildly disappointed that the information hadn't been conclusive.

After the men took their leave, Jan turned to Rose and Elaine. "If they *are* genuine, then who were Fredda and Tatiana?"

CHAPTER NINE

H ello, Dr. Tyson and Claudia!" Jan gave an enthusiastic greeting to the delightful couple. "I hope you've been enjoying this gorgeous day. Have you had a chance to look over the menu?"

"Hello, Jan," Claudia said warmly. Claudia was a beautiful African American woman, with pearly white hair pulled up in a loose bun and pearl drop earrings that looked like cream against her mahogany skin. She wore a simple peach cotton skirt and coordinating top with a summer jacket and a thin gold wedding band. Both husband and wife had a dignified air about them and the deepest warmth Jan thought she'd ever encountered in a couple.

Dr. Tyson McInnis wore an orange shirt that complemented his dark skin tone. He looked up with a grin that pleasantly smoothed the wrinkles on his face. The man was well respected as the town's former doctor, and the couple's son, Matt, and Matt's wife, Andrea, were the current doctors at Lancaster's Lakeview Clinic.

After chatting with Claudia and Dr. Tyson, Jan began to walk back to the kitchen with their order of honey-lemon

African Rooibos when Claudia called after her. "Send Rose out to say hello, will you? I haven't talked to that sweet girl in ages."

Jan almost stumbled. Claudia knew Rose? And for ages? That meant Claudia might have known Aliza too. "Will do, Claudia," Jan said, then scooted back to the kitchen.

Rose was pulling another batch of almond tassies from the oven when Jan said hello for Claudia. "She said she's known you for ages," Jan said, a statement, though she could hear the question in her own inflection.

Rose set the tray on top of the cool stove. "I loved going to Orchard Hill as a kid, and Mrs. McInnis babysat me sometimes. When I was little I thought she only came to see me." Face flushed from heat of the oven, she puffed away a strand of hair.

"Are you thinking what I'm thinking?" Jan looked knowingly at Rose.

"Yes, of course! If Mom opened up to anyone, it may very well have been Claudia."

"Did you have a chance to check with your mom's other friends to see if she told them anything about her past?"

"I called the two who came to mind, but they didn't know anything unusual about her. I never thought to ask Claudia because it's been so long since she was a daily part of my life."

"Well, she asked to see you."

"Aw, I didn't get to visit with her on Saturday." Rose dropped the oven mitts on the island and helped Jan fill the McInnises' orders. "Why don't you talk to her with me?"

Jan sent Rose on ahead to see the McInnises and then checked with Elaine to make sure she was fine handling the parlors. Then she joined Rose at the McInnises' table, where Rose had already explained the basics surrounding Aliza and the death certificates.

Claudia looked thoughtful. "Aliza never told me much." She dropped two sugar cubes into her teacup and picked up her teaspoon. "But a handful of times, after I'd watched you while she ran errands, she invited me to stay and visit."

"I told Jan and Elaine that Mom wasn't very social."

Claudia smiled. "She definitely was an introvert. She was precious. You and Clifton were her life, dear."

Claudia told a story of seven-year-old Rose, who'd wanted to bake her mother's birthday cake by herself. She'd fought Claudia's help, so Claudia pretended to look busy reading. When Rose was about to add two cups of cocoa powder to the frosting, Claudia stepped in to spare Rose from a sure disaster.

Rose was snickering by this point. "I had a stubborn streak. I was sure it would taste like hot cocoa."

"When I turned my back," Claudia said, her smile turning to laughter, "she emptied the whole cocoa container into the mixer bowl."

Rose grimaced and then joined in the laughter. "Mom still ate her whole piece and even most of the frosting."

As she wiped laughing tears, Claudia took Rose's hand. "Oh, she loved you." Claudia began another story from Rose's childhood.

Jan's gaze drifted down the street, where a man and a woman stood outside a storefront with their backs to her. She had no idea who they were or what brought them together, and she was struck by how much of life seemed random.

But too many details of this mystery were beyond coincidence, and she silently thanked God that He was in control of all of it. Not one detail had ever surprised Him. She pulled her focus back to the table conversation. "When was the last time you and Aliza talked?"

Claudia circled her spoon through her tea. "It must have been a year or so before she passed away. We kept in touch at holidays. She was never an open book, but at times she seemed to be hedging about something on her mind."

Rose's brow furrowed. "'Hedging.' That's how she was with me at times, but she'd always make an excuse about being distracted or busy."

"She did say something a couple of times that I never understood. Something like 'If only she'd made it' or 'If only I knew.' I could tell something had eaten at her a long time."

Rose looked bewildered.

"At times she seemed to be studying you, trying to figure out something. Not as if anything was wrong with you," Claudia assured her. "I couldn't put my finger on it, and she would never say anything about it."

Jan had almost forgotten Dr. Tyson was sitting next to her until he spoke around a toothpick. "Rose, don't let all this other stuff mess with your head. You knew your mom, even if you didn't know everything about her. Trust that."

Claudia nodded. "You'll figure it out. And it'll be okay, dear, even if it's hard. You've got your father, and also Elaine and Jan to help."

Jan thought Rose looked a little more peaceful as they both stood to get back to work. When Rose leaned down to hug

Claudia, Jan got another look at the couple down the street, this time facing her.

What on earth?

Allie McCall, the woman, was walking away from the much older man, and they headed to different cars. Jan thought she must need new glasses, but sure enough, Allie got into her yellow Beetle and drove away, and the man got into a charcoal-colored sedan and headed in the opposite direction.

Jan puzzled for a moment, trying to remember why the man looked familiar to her. And then it clicked.

Jan couldn't imagine what business Rose's renter would have with the unfriendly man who had shown unsettling and unwavering interest in Rose at the tearoom just a few days earlier. She would've pointed out the pair to Rose and the McInnises, but it was too late; Allie and the stranger were already in their cars, driving away. And Dr. Tyson looked ready to go. She'd mention it soon to Rose though. Maybe it was just a coincidence.

Even so, it was time to find out who that man was.

THE AFTERNOON PASSED quickly. By the time they started to clean up at 3:45, Elaine was ready to be done serving tea so she could get upstairs to look through the books from Rose's home. Clued in by Jan to the conversation with the McInnises and the fact that Allie McCall knew the older man from the tea, Elaine was champing at the bit to start fitting the pieces together.

Only two groups remained in the east parlor. Rose was wiping tables in the west parlor, and Jan was cleaning the kitchen while Elaine started to reconcile the receipts and the register cash.

A family of four with two pigtailed little girls was leaving. Before the door closed, a slender figure in a dressy shorts outfit slipped into the entry.

Elaine recognized the sleek-haired woman from Saturday and remembered her interest in writing a magazine feature about Tea for Two. She returned her guest's broad grin, which showed perfect white teeth. The books could wait. She wanted to talk with this woman.

"Hi there," she greeted cheerfully. "We haven't met but I heard you might stop in again. Lila Tate, right?"

The woman's dark eyes glistened, set off by her blousy royal-blue top. Elaine guessed her to be a few years older than Rose. A bracelet of dark metal links jangled when she flipped a lock of blue-black hair over her shoulder. "Yes. And you're...?"

"Elaine Cook. My cousin Jan and I own Tea for Two."

Lila looked apologetic. "I'm sorry to barge in at closing."

Elaine quickly gathered the paperwork on the counter and shut the register drawer. "No trouble. Actually, your timing's just about perfect. We were swamped today. Why don't you have a seat and I'll get Jan? We're glad you're here."

Since the east parlor still had customers finishing up, she showed the woman to a table in the west parlor, where Rose was going out the opposite door on her way to the kitchen.

"Rose, come meet Lila Tate."

Rose spun around, damp rag still in her hand. She looked surprised, but when she saw Elaine and Lila, she made her way toward them. She wiped her free hand on her apron and held it out to Lila. "Hi, Lila. Good to meet you." She excused herself and hurried back to check on the remaining patrons.

Elaine seated Lila and let Jan know she had arrived. With Rose ably covering the last tables, the cousins brought pots of chamomile and peppermint teas and a sample plate of pastries and sat down with Lila.

Elaine held out the snack plate. "Rue didn't say what magazine you write for."

"Oh. Right." Lila reached for a snickerdoodle and put it on her plate. "It's called *Lakeside Lights,* and I freelance for them. My editor agreed to see a piece about your tearoom."

"Why did you choose us?" Jan asked.

"It was pretty simple. They frequently highlight unique eateries in lake towns. My husband and I needed a vacation anyway, and we picked this area because I have an aunt who used to live in Maine. I remember visiting her as a kid."

"How lovely," Elaine said.

"We're always looking for new places on the water, and yours is just the kind they like. A start-up. Owners venturing in a new direction in life. A quaint waterside location. It's perfect."

"We're honored," Elaine said. "Just tell us what you need."

Lila smiled. "I'm thinking of writing it like a day in the life of a small-town lakeside business. So I'm hoping to sort of shadow you at some point. And do you ever share your recipes? I'd love to know how to make that kuchen. It would make a great sidebar in the article."

"Wasn't that good?" Jan answered. "We'll have to ask Rose. It was her recipe, a family one, I think. She might be willing to share it."

Elaine turned to Jan. "I think it would be all right, don't you? Having Lila shadow us for a bit?"

Jan nodded. "I don't see why not."

"Thank you! And if I promise to stay out of the way, could I come by sometime?"

Jan tipped her head. "You know, why don't we just do it now? It might be easiest if we show you around while we're still closing up. It's quiet. We can talk and ask questions. Then you can stop by anytime and observe when we're open tomorrow."

"Sounds good to me," Elaine said.

"That's actually perfect," Lila said. "Thank you."

"In fact," Jan continued, "you could help me with a new recipe I'm working on. It needs a little more tweaking, which I don't have much time for in the mornings."

Lila agreed right away, and they all moved into the kitchen. Lila was very friendly and asked questions about summer in Lancaster while Jan began pulling out ingredients and measuring cups and spoons.

"I've been wanting to update my molasses cookie recipe." Jan took an orange from the refrigerator crisper drawer while Lila stood at the island. "Last week I tried orange zest in the batter, but it wasn't really the pop I wanted. I'd like to try it again with a powdered-sugar glaze on top with a little orange extract in it."

Elaine never would have thought to combine molasses and orange and said so, admiringly.

"So Jan's the kitchen whiz, huh?" Lila asked, looking around again.

She seemed fascinated by the house and the kitchen, which Elaine appreciated, she supposed, and tried not to feel scrutinized. The more Lila took note of, the better the story ought to be. At least Lila wasn't obnoxious about it.

Lila looked caught off guard when Rose came back to the kitchen after the final cleanup, but she followed Jan's instruction and took the mason jar of baking powder from a cupboard.

"When will the story print?" Rose asked as she went to the office to put the register receipts on Elaine's desk.

"My editor said she needs it for the September issue."

They talked more while Jan ran the mixer. Lila's husband, Ray, was an architect, and they were thrilled to get away from the rat race for a little Maine-style R & R. Armed with spoons, the women all stood around the island and scooped dough balls on to the parchment-lined cookie sheets, chatting comfortably. While the cookies baked and Jan mixed the glaze, the cousins and Rose talked about the tearoom, explaining who did what and what their specialties were. Lila seemed interested in the deeper things as well, such as how all three women had ended up at Tea for Two because it was time for a new direction in life.

Suddenly, Lila gasped and pointed at the tablecloth folded on a far end of the counter. "Oh! Could I look at it?"

Rose hesitated but went to get it anyway, and Lila reached out to take it.

As she did, Elaine complimented her on the bracelet dangling on her wrist. It looked like an antique, its intricate design and links darkened with age. "How pretty..."

"This old thing?" Lila looked at it quickly with a dismissive shrug. "It was my grandmother's. It keeps falling off." As if on cue, the motion of her wrist shook loose the clasp.

They all laughed as Lila slipped the bracelet into her shorts pocket and focused on the tablecloth.

"Do you know about this kind of lace?" Jan asked her.

Lila had seemed excited about the tearoom, the cookies, getting to know Jan, Elaine, and Rose, but the lace seemed to hook her more than anything. "My grandmother was an expert seamstress."

She looked up at each of them. "Is this one of yours?"

"It was my mother's," Rose said.

"Did she make it?"

"She did," Rose said proudly.

The oven timer beeped just then, interrupting them.

"Here's the moment of truth," Jan said as she slipped on oven mitts and removed the cookie sheets from the oven.

All four women looked in consternation at the unappealing lumps of baked dough.

CHAPTER TEN

After locking the house, Jan had trudged upstairs with an armload of books. She knew that Elaine had also taken some books to her room. They'd said good night fifteen minutes earlier in pajamas and slippers and retreated to their rooms to read.

The long day finally rested under a blanket of darkness, and a nocturnal symphony of insects and frogs wafted in through Jan's open window. She sat up in bed with two thick pillows cushioning her back and her phone in hand. She had brought with her a couple of the books they'd borrowed from Rose's house, including a volume about the East German Stasi police. The unfortunate cookies had been taken out with the trash, and Jan's only guess about what went wrong was that Lila had grabbed cornstarch instead of baking powder. Easy enough to do. Both were powdery and white, and both had been stored in mason jars. They were marked, but Lila could have missed the small label. Oh well, she'd try again soon.

Aside from the baking disaster, it had been a nice way to end the day. Jan was excited about the magazine story, and even better was the fact that Lila knew about lace. Jan had meant to ask her more about that, but then they'd all ended up laughing and distracted about the cookies, and she'd forgotten. Lila might be just the person they needed to talk with. Maybe she could help Rose, once they got to know her a little better, of course.

She set the book down and navigated her phone's Internet browser to find the magazine's Web site easily enough. *Lakeside Lights* had an office in Vermont, and with a couple of screen taps, Jan saw Lila's name as a contributor. She read a couple of pieces Lila had written and liked the friendly tone of the writing and the publication in general. She'd be excited to tell her kids and friends to look for the Tea for Two feature in a couple of months. She could even see them hanging a framed copy of it on the wall behind the front counter.

Jan's thoughts wandered next to what Claudia McInnis had told Rose about Aliza. What had Aliza said?

"If only she'd made it."

If only who had made what? Tea? Kuchen? Something from lace? Or did "made it" refer to someone living or dying?

And *"If only I knew."* There were a million possibilities for that one.

Jan snuggled deeper into the covers. She spent a few more minutes browsing the Stasi book. She flipped to the index at the back and scanned through the *S* section. *Schultz, Georg.* He must have held a high rank to be singled out in a book about the entire regime.

The page that referenced Georg Schultz had been dog-eared. It included the same photo of him and his wife that had been in the newspaper clipping about their deaths. Jan stared at another small photo that was inset on an angle into the couple's picture. Although it had been a different view, she'd seen that house in Aliza's scrapbook. The caption told her it was the Schultz home in East Berlin.

She remembered that the photo in the scrapbook had obviously been taken with an inexpensive camera, a candid shot by someone with up-close access. *So there's your connection,* she thought grimly. It looked as if Aliza had known the Schultzes personally.

The page also included a photo of Georg in uniform standing in a concrete-block office. He certainly looked intimidating with a mustache that did nothing to make his stern face appear friendlier.

From the text Jan concluded that Schultz had been included in the book because he was known for being a particularly harsh official and for approving the deplorable conditions at the notorious Hohenschönhausen prison in Berlin. She stumbled as she tried to guess the word's pronunciation.

Suspicions still existed that his death and that of his wife, Berta, had not been accidental, but were acts of post–Cold War retribution by Western intelligence, although no specific country was mentioned and no proof had been found.

She flipped through the rest of the book. No other dog-eared pages and nothing else jumped out to her, so she put it aside and picked up the book about the art of European lace-making, which she figured would be more comforting reading before going to sleep.

Aliza had folded the corner of a couple of pages, and the first one Jan turned to described the Plauen tradition. According to a drawing of the country, the city of Plauen was in east-central Germany, near the border with Bavaria and the Czech Republic, some three hundred miles southwest of Berlin. Three photos of the town were included, and it looked as though it had the typical quaint European charm that Jan had seen in lots of pictures, although she hadn't traveled much. That had been Elaine's life.

Plauener Spitze, or Plauen lace-making, dated back to the fifteenth century. Pictures of machinery showed the modern way the lace was made. It had become a lucrative industry that had weathered plenty of storms, including high unemployment in town during World War I. However, in World War II, the town was bombed and fell under Soviet occupation, and the vast majority of the industry was destroyed.

In the 1950s, production resumed in Plauen, which by then was in Communist East Germany. Then in 1973, lace production was nationalized and family-run factories were taken over by the government. During German reunification after the Wall came down, privately owned factories were returned to their owners, and gradually the tradition was rebuilt once more.

On the nightstand, Jan's phone buzzed with an incoming text from Rose.

Talked with Dad. Will be in a little late in a.m. Hope that's okay.

Jan wondered if that meant Rose's talk with Clifton went well—or the opposite. But with a yawn, she realized she was too wiped out to think too hard about it. She pushed the books to the side of her bed and turned off the light.

THE NEXT MORNING Elaine was working in the office when Jan entered the kitchen to start baking.

"Morning," Elaine called from behind a stack of file folders. "Molasses on the menu today?"

"Oh, aren't you funny," Jan quipped at the teasing.

Elaine grinned. "Water should still be hot."

Jan thanked her and went to make herself some tea.

Elaine heard Earl Grey's meowing call for breakfast on the back porch stairs. She opened a tin of tuna, put it in a small bowl, and took it out to him. He approached cautiously, but soon his rough purr was sounding like one of the small motorboats that plied the waters of Lake Chickadee as he ate with obvious delight. Once he finished his meal, his eyes met hers for a brief moment. Still purring, he plopped down in a sunny spot to wash his face.

Elaine returned to her office, and while Jan began measuring and mixing ingredients for her famous chocolate chip peanut butter cookies, Elaine updated her on what she'd found from the books she had stayed up to look through. "The prison book I read wasn't for the faint of heart, I'll say," Elaine called out to Jan in the kitchen. "The Hohenschönhausen prison in Berlin was especially rough."

"Wow, that word rolled off your tongue."

"I practiced." Elaine joined Jan in the kitchen so they could talk without having to raise their voices over Jan's powerful stand mixer.

Jan smiled as she turned on the machine. She stood watching the dough fold over and over itself, then spoke. "I skimmed similar stuff about the Stasi."

"I'll spare you details," Elaine told her, "except to say that the book confirmed that it was the main prison for political prisoners and dissidents and was the Stasi headquarters in Berlin. When the Wall came down, Hohenschönhausen wasn't stormed by demonstrators like other government and military buildings were, so prison authorities had time to destroy evidence.

"Of course, we don't know whether Ernst Beck made it there or not. His letter was sent from Keibelstrasse, which was only a remand prison. He would have been sent there while awaiting his trial—for what, we still don't know. I looked for inmate records online but couldn't find anything."

Jan turned off the mixer and stirred in the chocolate chips by hand.

"But I did find one tidbit that may be helpful," Elaine continued. "In 1991 the reunified German government started allowing citizens to access their records."

"Which would be great," Jan reminded her, "except none of us are German citizens."

Well, there was that.

"I learned something about reunification too," Jan said and filled in Elaine on what she'd read about the lace industry and family businesses being taken over and then finally returned to their private owners, albeit in deteriorated condition.

"I've only owned one-half of this company for a couple of months," she added, "yet I can't imagine having it taken over. Livelihood gone. All those families lost a lot, and some of their factories had been theirs for generations."

Jan began scooping out even-size balls of dough from the mixer's bowl. Elaine helped her by rolling the dough balls in sugar and placing them in neat rows on the baking sheets. Then they gently pressed fork tines in crisscross patterns to flatten them into round discs, and the cookie sheets were ready for the oven.

As the time to open drew near, Elaine went to organize the food-drive items in the dining room and Jan washed the mixer bowl and started on double batches of blueberry corn muffins and bran muffins. She'd had her fill of molasses for a while. She'd also make a triple batch of toffee squares since those always went fast and were easy, and double batches of buried cherry cookies and buttermilk scones.

They made sure the tea service was prepared and then went upstairs to change into pants and light tops before the tearoom opened. Rose came in the kitchen door at twenty minutes before ten, which was earlier than Jan had expected. Her expression seemed lighter and less burdened than it had since the discovery of the death certificate.

"How'd it go last night?" she asked while Rose tied her apron.

"Better than the first time. Dad was surprised—I think genuinely—about Fredda's certificate. He said we'll talk more soon, but he got home late and was too tired last night. So it's a start. But that's actually not why I'm late. Someone's been spying on us again."

"Again?" Jan looked at her wryly. "Someone like Renter Allie?"

"Your guess is the same as mine."

"What happened this time?" Elaine asked her.

"When I got home yesterday I was walking around the house to water the garden out back and noticed a tree stump under a living room window." Rose's pause got the women to look at her. "Well, not really a tree stump. A log, turned on one end. Like from the firewood in the backyard. And the window-pane had been messed with, like someone had chipped at it to see if it was locked. Deputy Sheffield came out this morning and didn't find any fingerprints and couldn't get footprints from the grass. But it was obvious to him, too, that *someone* had rolled the stump to the house and also tried to get in."

"That sounds like more than a Peeping Tom, Rose." Elaine looked concerned.

Jan remembered what she'd seen down the street yesterday. "Rose, did you notice an older man here last Saturday? He wore a green shirt. Gray hair, gold watch...?"

"*Mmm*, no. Sorry. I was pretty distracted that day."

"I hadn't mentioned it because it slipped my mind and because you've had so much going on lately. But..."

Jan told Rose that the man had asked about her. She mentioned, too, that she'd seen the same man talking with Allie yesterday while she and Rose had been with the McInnises. "I was beginning to wonder if my imagination was getting the better of me, but you might want to talk with Allie. Or if you're not comfortable doing that, at least keep an eye on her if you can."

"How odd," Rose said. "This morning when she was leaving for work, I went out and asked if she'd seen anyone in the yard lately. She said no, no one except Jordy."

Jordy Quinn was Rose's twenty-year-old neighbor who often did yard work for them.

"She denied knowing anything about the stump. I couldn't tell whether she was lying. I guess I had no reason to believe otherwise. I even called Jordy to see if he moved the stump for some reason, and he said no. And I know I can believe him."

Jan didn't know what to make of it, but she was determined to find out who the mystery man was—if only she knew where to look for him.

The rest of the day passed unremarkably. It was a busy one on the lake, with boaters, fishermen, and swimmers enjoying the sparkling waters. The spicy and sweet scents of teas and pastries mingled with sunshine and coconut sunscreen as customers burst through the door in waves of chatter and laughter, then left cheerily a while later, heading back out to Chickadee Lake. The cousins took turns with Rose sweeping the floors to pick up the sand and pebbles left behind.

Before Jan could blink, it was six forty-five and she was walking down the stairs toward a grinning Bob Claybrook, feeling attractive in a way she hadn't felt in years. It wasn't a date, she'd reminded herself countless times over the last hour as she'd fussed with her hair, her earrings, her toenail polish, her outfit, her purse, her makeup, and her outfit again after Elaine shook her head and pulled something different from Jan's closet. If this wasn't a date, then whatever it was was deliciously exhausting.

"Wow, Jan." Bob actually reached for her hand and kissed it. Who did that anymore? "You look great."

The slimming silvery gray palazzo pants went perfectly with the short-sleeved, ice-blue sweater. Breezy and dress-casual, with a touch of "special," she hoped. Just right for this nondate.

She smiled back and took in the twinkle in Bob's eyes. He was looking good himself in a white linen shirt and navy pants with a contemporary cut.

They chatted easily as they passed his silver Acura MDX parked on the street and walked the short distance to the Hearthside Restaurant on Pine Ridge Road. The summer air wafted like silk over Jan's skin.

The Hearthside's upscale-rustic exterior carried into the interior. Large ceiling fans stirred the air, and tea lights flickered on white tablecloths around the large main room that was filled with diners. Waitstaff wore an urban look of black pants, starched white shirts, and straight black waist aprons and were taking orders in hushed tones. Rich aromas of seafood, steak, and garlic potatoes warmed the atmosphere, even without a fire blazing in the flagstone fireplace.

A host led Bob and Jan into an interior space with a handful of tables for two. Table candles and wall sconces provided the only light, which seemed just fine to the four couples who didn't look up from their conversations when Bob and Jan accepted menus from the host and sat down.

The prime rib didn't disappoint. A few minutes into their meal, Burk King, who owned the restaurant with his wife, Abby, stopped by their table to ask if they were enjoying the food. In their late forties, Burk and Abby wintered in Florida and operated the restaurant from Memorial Day through Labor Day. Their son, Tag, was a year-round Lancaster resident, a mechanic who owned the motorcycle-snowmobile shop and helped lead the Blizzard Riders snowmobile club as well as volunteered as a fireman.

Bob and Jan declared their meal superb, and Burk thanked them for coming and continued his round to the other tables.

The night was enchanting, and Jan had to remind herself as she swallowed a bite of bacon-wrapped asparagus that the whole purpose of this evening out—well, at least part of the reason—was so she could ask for Bob's help on Rose's behalf.

She sipped her drink before delving into that topic. "This has been wonderful, Bob."

He was chewing, but one side of his mouth curled up in an endearing smile.

"I wanted to tell you about our tearoom server, Rose, and her story and see if you can help me figure out where to go from here."

He listened as she quietly told him about the death certificates, the uncertainty about the names, Neal Danielson's tests, the adoption and Clifton's request to wait, the finds in the attic box, Aliza's knowledge of Plauen lace-making, and the books that had helped Elaine and Jan with historical facts.

She even shared what Claudia had told them about Aliza, about the mystery man who had asked about Rose and was still in town, and about Allie McCall's questionable behavior.

When she was done, she felt as if her burden had been lightened. "I don't know what it means for Rose, but if she could see her birth certificate from before Clifton adopted her, she might have an anchor or...I don't know." Doubt returned to wiggle in her gut.

But Bob was looking at her with admiration. And something more? He pulled the cloth napkin from his lap to wipe his mouth, then replaced it and rested his forearms on the table. "You were cute back in school, Jan Blake, but I never got close enough to realize how smart you are."

Her confidence lifted and she sighed with relief. She knew she was blushing, but she was okay with that.

Right now, this moment, it felt right.

CHAPTER ELEVEN

Elaine waited for a short time after Jan got home from her dinner with Bob, then knocked on Jan's bedroom door. She'd spent the evening curled up on the sitting room couch on the phone with Sasha, watching an old movie, and letting her mind wander where it wanted. It had been good to decompress for a few hours.

"Come on in."

Jan was sitting on her quilt-covered bed with a contented expression on her face. Aliza's tablecloth was draped across her lap. Her fingers moved gently over the lace, tracing the intricate pattern of the threads. An accent lamp on the nearby dresser sent a halo of light over Jan. Her silvery pants and solitaire earrings shimmered, and her blue eyes looked bright behind her lenses.

Jan sighed and gave Elaine a half smile. "Bob agreed to start the process of accessing Rose's birth records. He'll need her to sign off first, and it could take a few weeks."

Elaine started to nod, but ended up covering a yawn.

Jan pushed the tablecloth off her lap. "You need to get some sleep. Do you want to catch up tomorrow?"

"I wanted to hear how tonight went. You're glowing, by the way."

"*Mmm,* so I've heard. I had a nice time."

Elaine sat next to her cousin on the queen-size bed Jan and Peter had shared. She leaned over and kissed Jan's temple. "I'm really glad."

THE SUN HAD been up and the birds chirping for well over an hour when Patti Garland knocked on the front door of Tea for Two. Elaine swung open the door and greeted the young woman, who worked at the diner with her mom and older sister. "Hey, Patti, headed to work?"

"Mornin', Elaine. I've got the early shift but wanted to drop these off first. Love the food drive idea, by the way." Patti had the sparkly brown Pierce eyes, like Kate and Lydia.

Elaine took the two bags from her, and Patti hurried off. Elaine put the groceries in the dining room and then went to finish some orders at her desk while Jan baked the day's pastries. She savored the aroma of Jan's gingersnaps baking.

Elaine first pulled up her favorite online Bible site on her laptop and spent a few minutes focusing her heart and mind for the day.

As she was finishing, a motor rumbled out back and then shut off. Through the office window, she watched Rose climb out of the classic red motorboat and tie it to the dock post. Wondering why Rose was so early, Elaine joined Jan in the kitchen and poured three cups of lemon zinger tea. Jan held the door open for Rose, who came in dressed neatly in white denim capris and a purple polka-dot top.

She looked a little tired but smiled and dropped her purse on a kitchen chair, then accepted the tea from Elaine. She swallowed a sip and exhaled before looking at Elaine and Jan through watery eyes. "Mom wasn't my real mother."

Elaine's mouth felt dry. Jan looked incredulous.

Rose set her cup down on the island and reached for an apron. "I'm sorry to drop that on you right before we open, but…"

Elaine pulled her into a hug, and Rose cried for a couple of minutes. Jan stood nearby, a spatula hanging forgotten in one hand.

Rose suddenly pulled back and frowned, sniffing the air. "Jan, your cookies are burning!"

Jan turned quickly and snatched open both wall ovens. They were in luck. The white-chocolate macadamias survived, only a shade darker than usual, and the salvaged cookies lifted the tension.

"I've been saying I've wanted to know Mom better. I got my wish."

"So you had a good talk?" Jan washed her hands at the sink. "You and your dad?"

"We did." Rose looked composed again. "It was hard but good. I'm glad to finally know who she was."

"We want to hear all about it," Jan said, pulling out the three closest kitchen chairs.

When they were settled at the table sampling the fresh cookies, Rose summarized what Clifton told her the night before. "Mom was Fredda Beck. She grew up in East Germany, not Maine, and escaped across the Berlin Wall with her friend, who was my birth mother. I was born a few months later in West Germany. My birth mother died and gave my mom—Aliza—custody of me. That's when we came to America to be safe from my father's family."

Neither cousin said anything right away.

Rose took another drink. "There's more to it, and I'm not sure I can even remember some of the details right now. I was in shock listening to Dad tell me about it last night."

"How long has he known the truth?" Elaine hoped not long.

"Mom told him right before her surgery. He said she wanted him to tell me when the time was right, in case her surgery didn't go well." She looked dumbfounded. "I don't know if she had a sense that something would go wrong, but that's what she said to him."

"The other woman in the picture in front of the Plauen building—was that your biological mother?" Jan nudged the plate of cookies in front of Rose.

Rose took a bite of one and nodded. "It has to be her. I showed Dad the album and the letter from Ernst Beck. Ernst Beck was Mom's father. He and Mom's mother owned a lace-making factory, I assume the building in the picture. When the East German government took it over, he protested and was arrested by my birth father and grandfather, who were Stasi officers."

Elaine was glad Rose paused for a minute while the facts sank in. "So how did Aliza become friends with her father's enemies?" Up until now, she'd thought the death certificates were the most bizarre things she'd ever seen. Now she might be listening to one of the strangest tales she'd ever heard.

"After Ernst, that's Mom's father, was arrested and put in prison as a traitor, she and her mother were impoverished. Mom got a job as a nanny in a government official's home. The Schultz home, to be exact. Georg and Berta Schultz were my biological grandparents. Their son, Rolf, was my biological father, and his wife, Dagmar, was my birth mom and became Mom's good friend."

Jan pinched the bridge of her nose. "So the Schultzes are your birth family, and the Becks are your adoptive family."

"That's right."

"So how did Aliza and you come to America, and why the name changes? Where did *Sims* come from?"

Rose took a deep breath and looked at the ceiling. "The United States government."

Jan's head tilted.

"They wanted information on Georg Schultz because he was a high-ranking Stasi officer, and they knew Mom had lived in that house for several years and was close to the daughter-in-law, my...mother, Dagmar. When Dagmar died in prison, US officials came to Mom—Aliza—and offered her citizenship and birth certificates and a new start. You see, Aliza and Dagmar had become scared of Georg and Berta. Apparently Berta had accused Mom of stealing an expensive brooch Berta had given to Dagmar as a wedding gift. Dagmar defended Mom, and the brooch showed up soon afterward. But after the escape across the Wall, they worried that the Schultzes would come after them. They wanted Dagmar's baby—me."

Elaine felt confused. "But what about Rolf, your father?"

"He died right before Dagmar found out she was pregnant with me. It was some accident in the line of duty. Dagmar had been charmed by all of them for a while, long enough to marry my birth father. Over the years things got bad between my parents, but Rolf was still sort of a buffer between Dagmar and his parents. With him gone, Dagmar thought her in-laws would accuse her of things in order to take me from her. They'd already lost one grandchild—Rolf and Dagmar's son—a couple of years earlier. That's why Mom was already a nanny in the house before I was born."

"You had..." Jan's words trailed off.

Rose nodded. "Yes, I had a brother. Mom and Dagmar were also scared that the Schultzes would accuse one of them again of stealing the brooch. Mom told Dad that Dagmar thought Berta wanted the brooch back for herself. Dagmar had brought it with her in the escape, but Mom never knew where Dagmar hid it; Dagmar never told her in order to protect us until we could be safe from them. When Berta and Georg found us in West Germany, they did accuse Dagmar of theft, but this time of some silver items from their house as well as the brooch."

"Let me guess: they found the things in Dagmar's possession," Elaine mused.

"Just the silver platters, and that's why Dagmar was in prison. She was convicted of stealing those."

"Did Aliza—or Fredda—ever find the brooch?" Jan wanted to know.

"No. No one has ever seen it again, as far as we know. But Dad said at Dagmar's trial, she yelled for my mom to 'find it,' to 'look for it.' Mom figured that had to mean the brooch."

Jan went to get the teakettle to reheat their cups.

"Rose, did Aliza tell your dad what the brooch looks like?" Elaine asked.

Rose smiled. "This part I actually love. It's helping me process all the other stuff, most of all that my biological ancestors weren't very good people, except for my birth mom. The brooch was part of a set, a trio. The other two pieces are Dad's tie tack and my childhood pendant that we can't find. This is what's amazing: All three pieces originally came from the Beck home when Georg and Rolf Schultz ransacked it and arrested Ernst Beck. Nearly everything Mom's family owned was taken by those two officers. It was common practice during that time if someone stood up to the Communist government. Somehow Mom and her mom, Ane Beck, were able to hang on to the tie tack, which belonged to Ernst. Ane's brooch and Mom's childhood pendant were confiscated and became part of the Schultz possessions..."

"Which is how Dagmar came to own the brooch and why *Tatiana Rose* was engraved on the pendant. That's what she named you."

"Yes. Berta gave Dagmar both the brooch and the pendant—for a future granddaughter, which turned out to be me. Mom—Aliza—recognized it when Dagmar showed it to her for the first time after I was born. Dagmar returned it to Mom, but then Mom gave it to Dagmar and me anyway as a baby gift. She didn't have much money, and she told Dad that it meant a lot to her to give it to me since she and Dagmar had become so close. Then Mom had her birthstones swapped out for mine once she and I got to America."

"Wow." Jan exhaled the word.

"That's some news," Elaine stated as the facts were still catching up to her. "So Aliza kept those secrets to protect you from more trouble from the Schultzes."

"Sounds like she had good reasons to be concerned," Jan added.

Rose agreed. "It was a lot to hear, but at least I've got answers to a lot of my questions." She pushed away from the table and stood, then reached for their aprons hanging on nearby hooks.

Elaine thought it was going to take time for Rose to digest the fact that the mom she'd always known hadn't given birth to her.

The cousins took their aprons, and Jan carried the empty teacups and cookie plate to the sink.

They still had some time before the tearoom opened, so Rose helped Jan try making the molasses cookies again while Elaine returned to the office to finish the orders she'd meant to place before Rose arrived.

At ten o'clock she hurried to open the front door for Anita Picard, a selectman and owner of the I Scream Ice Cream stand, and Priscilla Gates. Each held a box of groceries for the food drive. Rose and Elaine stayed busy with customers through the morning.

During the lunch hour Bob called Jan to say his lawyer friend was willing to help. Jan told Elaine that to access Rose's birth certificate, Bob would have to go through the state registrar at the Department of Health and Human Services in

Augusta. And he'd ask a friend who handled adoptions to try to find Rose's adoption lawyer since his friend knew that group of attorneys in Maine. But, he pointed out, Clifton could easily answer those questions for Rose.

Finally, at ten minutes after four, the final customer left and Elaine locked the door. As they were cleaning up, she was surprised to see Clifton at the back door. He knocked and came in carrying two bags of deli sandwiches.

"Dad, what are you doing here? I was about to head home." Rose hugged him.

He and Jan and Elaine greeted each other warmly.

"I hope I'm not interrupting dinner plans," he began as Jan gestured to a seat at the table and he set down the bags of food. "I knew Rose might talk with you both today, and I wanted to check in to make sure you're doing okay, honey." He covered his daughter's hand with his own.

Rose assured her dad that she was fine.

"Thank you for bringing supper, Clifton," Elaine said.

When they were seated, he pulled several wrapped sandwiches and bags of chips from the bags and passed them around.

They talked about the election and their businesses, and when they were done eating, Clinton went to an attaché case Elaine hadn't noticed him carrying. He pulled a wrapped bundle from it and handed it to Rose. "After I got to the clinic this morning I remembered this of your mom's. For some reason I couldn't wait to give it to you, so I went home at lunch to get it."

A smile eased across Rose's face when she saw the white lace shoulder scarf inside the wrapping. "I remember this," she said in awe.

Jan was sitting next to Rose and helped her drape the scarf around her shoulders. "Your mother's work?"

Rose felt the scalloped edge of the lace. "I vaguely remember her wearing it once or twice." She showed them the two ends of the shawl, where Aliza had stitched three hearts on each end, and the initials *C, A,* and *R* in the hearts for their names.

"As far as I know, that was the last lace Aliza ever made," Clifton said.

They admired the scarf and then Clifton checked his watch. "I don't want to keep you, but I have one more thing to show you. Rose doesn't even know this yet because it came in today's mail, which I picked up when I went home. Rose, I brought it over because I thought you might like Jan and Elaine to see it too." He looked at the cousins. "Your support has meant a lot to her."

From his breast pocket, he removed an envelope, then unfolded the letter inside it. He looked it over and hesitantly handed it to his daughter, who looked back at him quizzically.

"Someone sent you a note in newspaper letters?" Rose tapped her fingers on her lips before reading it out loud. "WHERE DID SHE HIDE IT?"

CHAPTER TWELVE

The Youngs ended up staying at the tearoom until well after dark talking about what the note could mean. It was apparent that whoever sent the crudely lettered message knew there had been more to Aliza Young than she'd made public.

What wasn't apparent was how much he or she knew about Aliza's past. If it was someone from long ago in Germany, why send the note now, after all these years?

They threw away the supper wrappers and moved up to the sitting room with big mugs of tea. Clifton didn't want to impose and take more of their time, but Jan and Elaine both assured them it was no trouble and they wanted to help however they could.

"Thanks for being here for Rose. That's the biggest help. And honestly, I could use assistance figuring this out."

"It has to be about the brooch, right?" Rose asked, looking troubled. "Mom didn't have any kind of inkling about where the brooch was, even after she got here to the States?"

Clifton didn't have an idea what else it could be either. "Aliza seemed puzzled about how Dagmar expected her to find the brooch, and of course she never did. I don't think she had any more secrets. Her mood when she told me everything that night was one of relief, as if she was finally freed from all of it."

Aliza could have confided in someone else in America, even someone they'd considered a neighbor or friend. That person didn't need to know about the escape from East Germany, the threat from the Schultzes, or the American intelligence connection that brought Aliza and Rose to Maine. The only information necessary was that Aliza had mentioned something of value in her possession.

In the quiet of the sitting room, they traded ideas.

"Whoever sent that note thinks you're still keeping something hidden for Aliza." Jan tucked her feet under her in one of the chairs.

"That's right."

"It creeps me out that whoever it is doesn't have the character to talk to you directly, Dad." Rose scrunched her nose.

They all agreed that wasn't a good sign. Why the secrecy and anonymity?

The only reason Jan could think of was Aliza's recent death. When she was alive, had she somehow stood in that person's way to prevent him or her from making a move for the brooch? Or had her death triggered some clue that helped the person know where she was, where Fredda and Tatiana had been all these years?

The three faces before Jan were bright from the room's light, but through the slats of the window blinds blackness enveloped everything outside their small circle.

Someone was looking for something, and it involved Rose and her father. It had to be the brooch—what else could it be? But the Schultzes were dead, so who else would be interested in it? The stranger in the tearoom was Jan's first pick, with his question, and the way he watched Rose, and the fact that he'd talked to nosy Allie McCall. But a generally vague suspicion was all she had on him, and that wasn't nearly enough.

There was also Allie. What was she doing talking with the man? Was she really as innocently curious as she came across, or had she rented the Youngs' garage apartment for a more selfish purpose, maybe even a sinister one? She'd been caught snooping once; did she move the tree stump and mess with the window sash too? Was her questionable behavior related to the stranger from the tearoom?

A shiver shimmied up Jan's spine. Clifton was looking at her from across the room. Then he shook his head at something Elaine or Rose said. Jan was relieved he'd been honest with Rose. Jan had been hoping he'd prove trustworthy, not just for Rose but for Lancaster too, if he got elected.

Maybe Jan would talk with Claudia again and see if she'd remembered anything more about the years she was friends with Aliza.

Jan considered the value of the brooch, both monetary and sentimental. When the officers were taking Dagmar away in the courtroom, Dagmar would've been desperate for Fredda to protect her child—even more desperate than she would've felt over a diamond brooch, no matter how valuable it was. But the fact remained that it *was* valuable. Perhaps it had been sold to provide for Tatiana and Fredda.

"Clifton, did Aliza say much about when our government approached her? How did that connection happen?" Jan had been quiet for some time now, and the others looked surprised at the question.

Clifton shook his head. "She said she was approached in a park the day she learned that Dagmar had passed away in prison. Georg Schultz had been on our government's watch list for years, and they knew Aliza had lived in their house. They knew about the escape and Tatiana."

"Did she have contact with the government agents after she settled here?"

"It didn't sound like it, from what Aliza told me before her surgery. Why do you ask?"

"She probably spent a good amount of time with US officials during that whole process: the move, the name changes, answering all their questions about the Schultzes. I'm just wondering if somehow the brooch ended up getting misplaced in all of that red tape."

Jan didn't think Rose and Clifton liked the possibility any better than she did that the heirloom could be tucked away forgotten in a box in some government warehouse and none of them knew how to find it. "It would be a long shot, but so were a lot of the facts of Aliza's story."

"Have you looked for it much?" Elaine asked.

Clifton was already nodding before Elaine finished her sentence. "After Aliza told me the whole story I looked everywhere I could think of in the house."

"And we searched a few more places together last night. The cupboards, the garage, her desk, her closet," Rose said.

"No safe deposit box number showed up?" Elaine asked.

"Nothing." Clifton shrugged unhappily.

ELAINE ENTERED THE kitchen early Thursday morning in her flowered pajamas and robe, still thinking about their talk last night. She helped herself to a steaming cup of English breakfast tea before going in search of her cousin.

"I think Clifton should show Deputy Sheffield the anonymous note. He already knows about the stump and the window," she said as she walked out on to the screened porch, where Jan sat with her Bible on her lap. "Now the note . . ."

"They seem connected."

"They do. And there could be fingerprints on the paper."

"Except that so many of us handled it yesterday," Jan said with a wry smile. "Still, I think he ought to show it to Deputy Sheffield." She covered a yawn.

"I didn't sleep well either." Elaine caught Jan's yawn-bug and held back one of her own.

"I woke up thinking about the selectmen debate tonight. It seems like an interruption in Rose and Clifton's family business."

"I guess you didn't hear Clifton talk about that last night. He isn't too worried about it." Elaine pulled her robe around herself and took a seat on the other wicker chair. "He's probably got so much on his mind that it didn't occur to him to call the sheriff."

Jan looked skeptical. "I hope he can do that discreetly. The last thing they need is someone to get wind of all this and blow it out of proportion."

"I don't know the man, and I don't want to judge, but I wonder if J. Eisley Segouri wouldn't be above that kind of thing."

"Let's hope not. I think most of the town would show common sense and not assume Clifton's got anything to hide." Jan set her Bible on the table between them, picked up her teacup, and listened as Elaine spoke her thoughts.

"I was also thinking about Neal's tests on the certificates. He was right when he said they weren't made by an amateur. I'll call Nathan later."

"Do you think Clifton told Rose everything? I mean, he only told her about Aliza because Rose pushed him a little." Jan adjusted her glasses.

"He said he was still figuring out how to help her through it. He was protecting her, so who knows if he still is?" Elaine went on to question whether Rose's West German birth certificate still existed, since that would have been her true original one. "And do you think there's any way to find out about the American intelligence thing?"

Neither cousin had an idea at the moment.

After changing the subject to talk about some business expenses, the food drive, and the holiday events that would begin the next day, Elaine went upstairs to shower and get ready for customers.

When the tearoom opened, Elaine visited with Jack Weston, the game warden, who came in for a cup of black tea to go before heading out to the lake to check fishing licenses and enforce boating regulations. Tall and in his early thirties with light brown hair and blue eyes, Jack was both friendly and frank. These qualities, along with his boyish grin, made him a favorite among the younger lake-goers, who looked for the ice cream coupons he handed out to kids who wore their lifejackets properly.

"See you tonight, Jack?"

"Wouldn't miss it. I'm sure it'll be a hoot." Raising his to-go cup in farewell, Jack grinned and left.

Linda Somes, the town manager, also breezed in on her break. Elaine knew she'd see Linda at the debate. Linda remained close-lipped about her thoughts on either candidate, and Elaine respected that. There'd be enough drama at the Old Grange Community Theater that evening. The debate between Clifton Young and J. Eisley Segouri was scheduled for seven o'clock.

During lunch Rose decided that Clifton would want to know her plans to see her pre-adoption files. She paused midbite to send a text to that effect, and to ask her father's help in tracking down the adoption attorney. "We might know the lawyer's name in a few minutes. I told him I'll explain later and it's all good."

Jan held a forkful of rice. "Is your dad ready for tonight?"

"I think so. He seemed good this morning. He did tell me to be careful though"—Rose stilled her glass at her lips—"and he wasn't talking about watching out for traffic. We're both looking over our shoulders a little more."

"I think I'll ask around whether anyone's renting to our mysterious male stranger," Jan said thoughtfully. "Someone has to know who he is."

Elaine suggested Ned and Rue Maxwell and also thought Des or Jo Murphy might have seen him in their store.

"Kate Pierce too," Rose added. "He has to eat somewhere."

Jan also added Burk and Abby King from the Hearthside to their list of people to question.

"I suppose we should ask Macy too," Elaine said with a groan, which brought a laugh from Rose and Jan.

Jan's phone pinged with an incoming text from Bob. He had papers to run by the tearoom for Rose to sign.

Rose's phone pinged too. "Dad says the lawyer's name was Simon Pelletier, and he still practices in Augusta."

Jan sent Bob the lawyer's name, and Bob replied offering to make the preliminary contact with Mr. Pelletier. It would be wonderful to have another source who might have known more about Aliza's past.

Things actually felt like they were moving along in some ways, Elaine thought.

At three thirty Bob met with Rose in the kitchen. He'd spoken to Simon Pelletier about the papers and would e-mail them to Simon, who'd take it from there with the registrar at the Department of Health and Human Services. Rose should expect it to take several weeks, but Simon would request an expedited process. And he had his paralegal pull the Young papers from his archives, which he would scan and send to Bob.

Elaine was at the counter saying good-bye to a group of elderly women when Rose and Bob came up front. Bob had the file tucked under his arm, and within a few weeks Rose would get her first look at her first American birth certificate.

Not many people had two birth certificates, much less three. Someday it would be nice if Rose could have a look at her very first one, from West Germany.

Rose was greeting a couple and Jan was saying good-bye to Bob, so Elaine brought the broom to sweep the front porch one more time. She finished the steps and was on her way back inside when a small flash of white and black caught her eye. A scrap of paper was sticking out from beneath the welcome mat. She was about to drop it into the trash can behind the counter when she looked closer.

It was a black-ink newspaper *A*. She went back out to the porch for another look, and sure enough, there was another one, a *Z*.

Bob and the late-afternoon customers left, and as soon as the door was closed and locked, Elaine showed Jan and Rose the letters from the porch. If Clifton hadn't just received the odd note made of newspaper cutouts, these two scraps would've landed in the garbage without a second thought.

"Why would an *A* and a *Z* be on the porch outside the tearoom?" Rose voiced the obvious.

"My guess is the person who sent that note to your dad had cut out a bunch of letters," Jan suggested.

"And maybe changed the message. Or maybe was planning another one, with the word *Aliza* in it."

"I don't guess it was a kid doing an *A*-to-*Z* alphabet project for summer school."

The cousins grinned. But one thing seemed clear, and it unnerved all of them: whoever sent the newspaper note to Clifton had been in the tearoom not long ago.

CHAPTER THIRTEEN

Jan and Elaine entered the Old Grange Community Theater a few minutes before seven. Fifty or so people were already there mingling with their neighbors. Jan waved to Bob, who had saved seats for them.

Up front in the auditorium Clifton and J. Eisley were in suits and ties, seated in chairs to the left of a wooden podium. Jan noticed that Clifton wore his tie tack. To the candidates' right, two chairs were reserved for Mark Payson, the town clerk and tax collector, and Linda Somes, the town manager who'd been to the tearoom earlier in the day.

On the other side of the podium the current selectmen, Chairman Eldon Carter, and Alan Oakley, Anita Picard, and Julie Yeaton were seated in a row, talking together.

Each of the selectmen served for three years. They met once a month, or more if needs arose. Their jobs made the town run smoothly. They hired town officials and listened to residents' complaints, and they managed bids for road repair and maintenance in town.

The sole purpose of this meeting was for the residents of Lancaster to hear from the two candidates about their vision for the town.

River White and Candace Huang, reporters for *The Penzance Courier,* were taking notes already. River had a reputation for always getting his story, even though—or perhaps because— he could be a nuisance. Candace, on the other hand, seemed more approachable.

Promptly at seven o'clock, Eldon Carter welcomed everyone and led them in the Pledge of Allegiance, and then launched into the reason for the meeting and the responsibilities of a selectman. He introduced the four currently serving, and then J. Eisley and Clifton offered a few words about their backgrounds as residents of Lancaster. Each man had ten minutes to say whatever he wanted about himself and his family, his qualifications, and what he'd do for the town if elected.

While Clifton was talking, Jan looked at the faces around her and wondered if anyone there had sent the note. She knew she could trust Bob, Elaine, and Rose. She *thought* she could trust her closest neighbors. But what if one of them had sent the note? What if the note wasn't about the brooch? What if it was political in nature? If so, what had the sender wanted?

When Eldon opened the meeting up for questions, it didn't take long for divisions to show up. The town was split between the old and new. Even Elaine added her voice for Clifton, saying she didn't see any reason to raise the taxes on the town's small businesses because the town was already flourishing, and it would put too much strain on the owners and actually hurt the downtown.

Jan was proud of her cousin's chutzpah. Elaine seemed unfazed by disapproving looks from J. Eisley supporters. As Jan bumped shoulders with her cousin, she caught the eye of a newcomer in the room and quietly gasped.

The mystery man she'd been looking for was standing by the wall near the back, partially tucked behind some other people. Although his dark gray hair and face probably went unnoticed by the crowd, he stood out like a beacon to Jan. He seemed to be looking from Clifton to Rose, who was seated on Jan's other side.

What was his interest in the Youngs? Jan's thoughts raced, and the debate faded into the background. Had he sent the note to Clifton? If so, why? His focus on Clifton and Rose was obvious, and Jan wondered if Elaine saw what was going on behind the scenes.

The man looked at her again, and she fought the urge to turn away. Instead, she raised a questioning eyebrow at him, not caring if it seemed rude.

His expression remained stoic, but he looked away, and Jan watched him nod to someone else. Bianca Stadler from the Pine Tree Grill was waving to him from her perch near the opposite wall.

So he knew Bianca. Jan would need to speak with her as soon as possible. But first, after this meeting was over, she'd approach the man.

The minutes wore on from that point. Darby Clement, the road commissioner, was arguing, running roughshod over someone else who was supposed to have the floor, and it took Eldon several minutes to shush the townspeople.

Finally, when the meeting was adjourned, Jan leaned toward Bob and Elaine. "I'll catch up with you in a few minutes." Before they could respond she scooted through the moving group of people toward the spot where the man had been standing.

As she got closer, she saw him slip out the back door. She balled her fists at her sides. As she stood in the doorway between the lighted room and the darkening outdoors, she felt someone come up behind her. She gave a start, but Bianca Stadler placed a hand on her arm.

"I didn't mean to startle you, Jan," she said with her characteristic wide grin. Fifty-something Bianca was one of the owners of the Pine Tree Grill, a place Jan and Elaine had come to really enjoy in the past few months.

Sturdily built with long brown hair and always in full makeup, Bianca wore gold bracelets that jangled like wind chimes as she gestured toward the street. "Not the friendliest one, is he?"

"You do know him, then? I saw you wave to him."

Bianca looked dubious. "Well, I wouldn't say I know him, but he's been in the Grill a couple of times this week. Tight-lipped for sure. Said his name is Thomas Spence."

Thomas Spence. Jan made a mental note. "Do you happen to know why he's in town?"

"Not really. He told me he's in pharmaceutical sales." She held her hands up and her bracelets clinked.

"Any idea where he's staying?" Jan asked.

"He mentioned a hotel in Waterville. I don't know which one."

After inviting Jan to come by the Grill soon, Bianca went to find her brother, and Jan looked for Bob and Elaine.

She caught sight of Matt McInnis standing with his wife and parents and got an idea. The room had cleared some by then, so she was soon at their sides. After hellos, Jan asked Dr. Matt if any pharmaceutical reps had stopped by his clinic that week. "I know it's an odd question…"

"No, it's been pretty quiet, Jan. Why do you ask?"

"I heard there's a new rep in town and wondered if he'd made the rounds to you yet. I'm surprised he hasn't since yours is the only doctor's office and he's been in Lancaster almost a week."

The younger Dr. McInnis smiled good-naturedly. "Maybe he's fitting in some fun before business."

Jan chuckled and agreed that was good practice. She visited with the four McInnises another minute before rejoining Elaine, Bob, Rose, and Clifton. After some chit-chat, Bob said he had to leave and Jan walked with him to his car. When she got back to the Youngs and Elaine, she heard Clifton saying he'd taken the note to Arnie Sheffield, who would run fingerprints on the letter and the envelope.

She complimented Clifton on the debate and then thought of one more question. "Do you remember where the envelope was postmarked?"

"I do. Deputy Sheffield noticed it. It was sent from Waterville."

CHAPTER FOURTEEN

Elaine was just returning from an early Friday morning walk, observing her fellow shop owners rolling out display racks and setting up tables for sidewalk sales, when she encountered Jan coming around the side of the house. "It's strange, Elaine," Jan commented without preamble.

The cousins had already carried several plastic bins from the attic and grouped them in the front yard, then set up an easel and a food-drive sign next to the bins. They'd lugged a folding table outside and set it up next to the easel.

Jan was dressed in her moss-green Victorian costume and red-white-and-blue mobcap. After Elaine showered and dressed in her costume and cap, they would bring out a couple of large glass urns with spigots to serve iced tea to customers or anyone stopping by with food donations.

Earl Grey ventured around the edge of the porch to see what all the activity was about. He picked his way to the driveway, where he sat down, looked at the cousins with studied disinterest, and began to concentrate on licking his paw.

"Yes, the Thomas Spence situation is strange," Elaine agreed as she arranged a stack of drinking glasses on the table. "But Rose and Clifton haven't ever seen this man who watches them, avoids conversation, is staying in Waterville where the newspaper note was mailed to Clifton, and who is a pharmaceutical rep that hasn't bothered to stop in to sell his meds at the one medical office in town. I'm sure he has a good explanation," she added humorously.

"He's got an agenda, that's for sure," Jan said as she twitched the edge of the tablecloth into place, "but I'm not sure selling pharmaceuticals is it. Is there much going on in town yet?"

"Yep. You need to sneak out sometime and see what's happening." She told Jan about the shops spilling out on to the sidewalks and the farmers' market filling up with artisan booths and produce from local growers. "The Richardsons have some imported cheeses for sale and samples of chocolate milk. The ice cream stand has a line already, and the McInnises are selling vegetables and peaches. Oh, and I scored a piece of breakfast sausage when I passed the Grill. Mel was handing them out."

It was nine o'clock, and the sun had dried the dew from the grass, by the time the first car pulled up and parked by their display. Dark-haired Lydia Pierce got out, eyes sparkling, and handed the cousins that week's edition of the *Weekly Wave*. "Check out your food-drive ad. Hopefully it'll help your efforts!" She returned to her car and called out for help with two restaurant-size cans of tomato sauce and a case of spaghetti noodle boxes in her trunk.

As Lydia was pulling away, Jo Murphy walked up carrying a case of paper products, which Jan thanked her for. Thin and curly-haired, Jo was married to Desmond Murphy, and they owned the general store across the street from Tea for Two. The one-story building had been in their family for more than fifty years, and Des and Jo planned to hand it down to their teenage sons.

"Des and I missed the meeting last night," Jo said, looking mostly at Elaine in a way that made Elaine know something else was behind Jo's words. Energetic and with a big heart, Jo wasn't nosy but couldn't help picking up news and town gossip in her busy store.

"It was something, that's for sure," Elaine admitted, shaking her head.

"So I heard." Jo lowered her voice and tucked a light-brown lock behind her ear. "I hope business is good for you today." When Elaine sent her a quizzical look, Jo went on. "Diane Blanchett's nephew came in the store a while ago and bought several boxes of tea from us because he, quote, 'didn't care for your views' and didn't want to have to get tea by coming here. 'Your views' being Clifton's. He heard your comments at the meeting last night and said he doesn't want this town held back by people who supported 'outdated ideas.' I know one person won't make much difference. But still, I hope his attitude doesn't spread."

Elaine was frustrated. "Me too. I'm sure most people will show more common sense."

"Agreed." Jo gave a firm nod. "By the way," she continued, looking at Jan this time, "put aside a couple dozen of anything for me later today, will you? We have family coming for the weekend, and I won't have time to bake. Oh, and we've got more napkins and paper towels for the drive. Des'll bring them by later."

After Jo left, Elaine helped Jan bring out boxes of cranberry-orange scones and cherry-cheesecake brownies, and white paper bags of oatmeal-raisin, chocolate chunk, and mini maple croissants. She plunked them down on the table one by one, with emphasis, until she caught Jan's look. "Sorry."

"Don't tell me you're letting one comment from some guy who doesn't even know you get under your skin."

Elaine was about to answer when a black BMW SUV with a boat trailer hitched behind it pulled up and Lila Tate and her husband got out. Both wore white visors and were dressed for a classy day on the water. Lila's hair swung from a sleek, low ponytail through the visor's back strap, and she flashed a smile as her floral perfume wafted in the air. "Hey, Elaine and Jan. We come bearing gifts!"

The couple added several bags of groceries to the bins, and Lila introduced Ray, whom they hadn't officially met. He handed Elaine a folded newspaper. He seemed nice enough, but he had a reserve about him, unlike his friendly wife.

Ray nodded to Elaine to look at the paper. It was today's *Penzance Courier*, and the leading headline read "Town Divided over Election." She almost missed it because the accompanying picture was large and she was in it.

With mixed feelings, she scanned the first couple of paragraphs of the story. It appeared that River White had slanted the piece somewhat in favor of J. Eisley and had also featured a quote from Elaine's spirited comments.

She looked at Lila and Ray and felt Jan's uneasiness. She was not about to give in to River White's fight-picking, although inside she felt a spotlight glaring on her. "He certainly created a story, didn't he?"

Lila wrinkled her pert nose. "We've been reading the papers the past few days because we're thinking of buying a summer home on the lake. We've just fallen in love with the area," she gushed. "We're not sure what to make of this election drama, although I suppose politics can get messy anywhere."

Elaine wanted to change the subject. "How's *your* story coming along?"

Lila tilted her visor back. "It's good. I'm hoping to spend some more time here in the next couple of days. It's hard fitting in work when there's so much fun going on." She smiled.

At that moment Rose walked up from the back. Her hair hung loosely around her shoulders and she looked freshly windblown.

"Morning, Rose. Drive the boat again?"

Rose dropped her purse to the grass and said hello. "It's easier on my old car this way." She grinned. "And more fun."

"You've met Lila Tate, of course," Elaine said to her. "This is her husband, Ray."

Rose swept up her hair and twisted it into a clip, then held out her hand. "Rose Young. Pleased to meet you. I think I've seen you around."

Elaine couldn't miss the look on Lila's face, though it was quickly replaced by her usual smile. What it meant, however, she didn't know.

Rose turned to Jan to ask what she should handle in the kitchen before they opened. "Oh, Jan and Elaine, Dad and I want to know if you'd like to eat with us at the barbecue tonight. A boat ride's included. Ray, Lila, you'd be welcome too." She looked at the boat hitched to their vehicle. "If you're not tired of the lake by then."

Jan agreed enthusiastically, and Elaine nodded. Lila caught Elaine's look and pulled her attention back to the tearoom tables and donations.

"I want to come by later for more cookies. I can't get enough of them," she said.

"Anytime. We'll be here. We'd love to see how your story's coming along."

Ray reached for his wife's arm. He seemed ready to go, but Elaine could see Lila was still glancing subtly at Rose as she jogged up the front steps of the tearoom.

"Oh, Lila, I almost forgot." Jan stood up straight from where she'd been arranging the to-go bags. "When you have time, I'd like to pick your brain about lace. What your aunt taught you about it."

Lila looked surprised. "Oh, of course."

Another glance from Ray. Maybe he was just the nervous type, Elaine thought.

Elaine walked them to their car, and they drove off with the boat trailer following behind.

She turned back to Jan. "I thought her grandmother was the seamstress. Wasn't it her aunt she used to visit?"

Jan bent to pick up something from the grass. "Oh, look. Her bracelet fell off. She'll be back for this." She looked perplexed as she watched the SUV turn the corner. "Yeah, I thought so too. I'm sure she was just being polite. That must have been why she seemed confused at first by my question."

Elaine glanced at her watch as she unrolled the newspaper still in her hand. Twenty after nine. She still needed to shower and change into her Victorian garb. The display looked ready for business, and on her way up to the house, she took another look at River White's article.

As her foot hit the top stair of the porch, someone called to her from the sidewalk. She turned to see River himself coming toward her with a reporter's searching grin plastered across the freckles on his face.

"Is Rose in yet? I'm doing another story about the candidates. You know, really help readers get to know them." He looked purposeful and nosy, and his grin broadened. "I want to make sure my reports are balanced, so I'd like to talk to her about her parents."

CHAPTER FIFTEEN

Miss Young, I couldn't get much from your dad this morning," River was saying when Jan walked up to the front of the tearoom. He was dressed in khakis and a blue polo shirt and held a recording device.

Rose and Elaine stood nearby, and Elaine looked annoyed. The oven timer would go off in four and a half minutes, and without knowing any details of why River was there, Jan was already hoping he'd be gone before the scones were done.

"I'm having trouble finding out much about your mother, Aliza. I understand she recently passed away. I'm sorry to hear about that." Jan thought River's smile looked disingenuous.

"Yes, we miss her." Rose had just come downstairs after changing into her rose-colored period dress, and she wasn't forthcoming with information.

"I'm sure the voters would like to know more about Dr. Young's family, and you're a good person to talk to, being his daughter and all. Clifton adopted you, right? Could you tell me how your mom and dad met?"

Rose looked uneasy. River's questions were blunt and unwelcome. If Jan were a betting woman, she'd place high stakes that River White didn't care about helping Clifton or Rose. He was always after a story, even if it meant butting into Rose's or Clifton's personal business.

Rose cleared her throat. "I'm really not interested in talking with you, Mr. White. I'm sorry. We had a great family life, and we're still adjusting to her being gone. I think that's all voters need to know."

"River"—Elaine stepped forward and practically turned him around to the door—"we're opening soon, and I'm sure you have more interesting leads to follow up on, so we'll say good-bye now."

River moved toward the door without more prodding, but before Elaine closed it after him, he looked back at Rose one more time. "Call me, Ms. Young, if you care to help your father."

The women stood there until River's car rumbled to life and he drove away.

Rose shook her head. "I've got to finish refilling napkins."

Jan checked her watch and headed for the kitchen, and Elaine went upstairs to get ready. Walnut scones were cooling on racks, blending their aroma with licorice tea that Jan was pouring into three cups. The timer beeped, and she took out more trays.

She knew River's questions hit close for Rose. When Rose came into the kitchen, Jan patted her shoulder.

Rose gave her a quick hug. "I'm fine. Thank you."

"Don't worry about River White. He's going to write what he writes."

Worry still needled at Jan a little, though she wouldn't say so to Rose. She didn't like River's patronizing tone, as if the town—or at least he—was owed a detailed explanation of Clifton's life. It was a selectman campaign, for goodness' sake. Not the country's presidency.

She really didn't care for J. Eisley Segouri, and the thought of a behemoth Seg-Way store within throwing distance of her home and business nauseated her. But any trouble River stirred up for the Youngs would only make it harder for them to get on with their lives, which they were trying hard to do.

Jan wasn't sure what to expect in the morning's paper. She wondered if River was digging into J. Eisley's life as much.

Rose took her cell phone from her pocket. "I'm going to let Dad know River stopped by."

She took her phone into the secluded dining room, and Elaine entered the kitchen wearing her floor-length blue costume. Jan helped her secure her mobcap with one more bobby pin and quietly told her that Rose was talking with Clifton.

Elaine reached for a scone and broke off a bite, then reached for another one and gave it to Rose, who had come back into the kitchen.

"Dad was reassuring, but I could tell he's trying to make me feel better. He reminded me that we're not hiding anything. We're just working through some new information."

Jan picked up a scone for herself, not caring that they were eating their profits. "It isn't anyone's business. And neither one of you knew your mother's story until very recently. The majority of people in this town won't care."

Elaine looked thoughtful. "But you know, it might not be a bad idea to have a response ready in case you don't like what River writes."

Rose looked interested. "What do you have in mind?"

Jan let the warm scone slip down her throat as they waited for Elaine to explain.

"What if you and your dad talk to another reporter? Candace Huang, for instance? You might even consider telling her a few things about your mom."

Jan drew in a breath. "*Ooh*, that's good. You'd keep the control."

"Exactly." Elaine clicked her tongue and popped another bite of scone into her mouth. "Take back the element of surprise River's itching for."

Rose tipped her head as if she was considering it. "You want me to tell her my family's private business? What are the chances anyone will believe, in all the years they were married, that Dad really didn't know about my mom? It raises more questions, even to me, and I know him enough to trust him."

Jan gave her a conspiratorial smile. "That's exactly why you and your dad might want to talk to her. Do it on your own terms."

Elaine nodded, looking hopeful. "She'll write you a good story, Rose." She rubbed her hands together eagerly. "That is, if you're ready."

Rose reached again for her phone. "I'll see what Dad thinks." She went back to the dining room.

Jan dropped the bracelet on the counter. "Remind me to give that back to Lila."

Elaine reached for it. "This is beautiful."

"It is. And she seems nice. But I think she's pretty new at interviewing. I'm surprised she hasn't asked us more questions yet."

"Yeah, but I'll take her style over River's any day."

Rose came back and confirmed that her dad agreed to talk with Candace Huang, but only after he saw River White's story.

The day passed busily as Jan and Rose worked together in the kitchen, and Rose and Elaine tag-teamed to help customers inside and out. At noon they all changed back into normal clothes because the long dresses had become uncomfortable in the day's full heat. At one point in the afternoon, Jan came outside with more baked goods, and Elaine commented about the pace. "If this keeps up, we'll need more help every day."

"I like that problem, especially considering the dire warnings we've heard lately." From the porch, Jan could see campaign signs posted along Main Street.

When she returned to the kitchen, she found that Amy had texted to see if she wanted to meet up with Van, the boys, and her at the chicken barbecue, and Jan happily agreed. Bob had mentioned seeing her too, and Jan looked forward to spending a fun evening as a group.

With the crowds out enjoying the town's events, the stores stayed open later than usual, including the tearoom. Jan, Elaine, and Rose were just starting to shut things down at five o'clock when Van parked their white Honda Odyssey minivan in front of the tearoom and helped dismantle the display and take the table and easel back into the house until the next day. He also brought in a couple of paint cans in the color the cousins had chosen for the office and said he and Brian would find time to fix their kids' wallpaper mishap soon. The women and twins brought the bins inside, and the boys leaped up the stairs, shouting about beating each other to the tower room.

They had everything put away and cleaned up by five thirty. Rose went outside to meet her dad, who was parking his car in the driveway, and Amy called the boys downstairs.

"They've been up there this whole time?" Jan asked with a laugh. She couldn't imagine what was so interesting on the near-empty, dusty third floor, but most kids had great imaginations and she knew her two grandsons were no exception.

"We were playing pirates," Max boasted when they reached the main floor.

Jan laughed and led the way out the door, thinking she needed to give the house some attention soon, including a good cleaning. But that would have to wait. Right now she was hungry and ready to see Bob.

CHAPTER SIXTEEN

From the edge of the crowd outside the Pine Tree Grill, Elaine waved to Bob, who had already arrived at the barbecue. Cars and bikes filled the street spaces. Music from a live band drew the partygoers to a common area.

Small American flags were propped in mason jars on the sea of long tables, and larger flags fluttered around the eating area. Dozens of people already had plates loaded and were finding places to sit. The air was warm, and on the lake boats were kicking up waves in every direction.

Elaine's stomach growled as she smelled the chicken cooking and the corn ears boiling in huge stainless steel pots on grills set up along an outside wall of the restaurant. Several kitchen staffers helped Mel Stadler man the grills. Bianca was nowhere to be seen for the moment, and Elaine hadn't seen Clifton or Rose since Rose had gone home.

She followed Jan and her family through the crowd to the table Bob had claimed and felt a twinge of nostalgia for her kids and grandkids as she watched Jan introduce Bob to Amy, Van, and their boys. She smiled to herself though. She was happy for Jan.

"Hi, Elaine," someone said behind her. She turned at Nathan's voice.

"Hey there, Nathan. I didn't expect to see you here." Nathan didn't live in Lancaster. Content to let Jan enjoy her family, Elaine sat down with Nathan to catch up on the week.

"Any news from Neal?" she asked. She'd called him to tell him about the US intelligence part of the mystery. Nathan said he'd let Neal know and ask if that shed any more light on the certificates.

"That's actually why I came tonight. He called with the results this afternoon." Nathan removed his sunglasses and his eyes twinkled bluer than usual with the lake behind him. "He didn't find anything questionable about either one. They're 'either genuine or fake but the impeccable work of professionals.'" He emphasized the words as though he was quoting directly.

"That's because our own government made them."

He dropped his sunglasses on the table. "Crazy, isn't it." It was a statement more than a question.

"Could he tell us anything more about them after knowing they're American made?"

Nathan shook his head. "Sorry."

"I figured as much. Thanks for the help." She told him about River White's questions and the strange newspaper letters on the tearoom porch.

He took a swig of Coke, then teased, "You've got another full-fledged caper on your hands."

"I know," she bantered back. "Jan and I are getting to be professional grade. And we thought we'd just be serving tea into old age."

He chuckled. "Well, I'm here to help anytime. Don't hesitate to ask."

Just then Rose and Clifton walked up to the table. Everyone welcomed them, and for the next hour they were able to relax and have a good time. Teenage servers in shorts and patriotic T-shirts came around with buckets of corncobs, more chicken, rolls, and drink refills while the band played song after song.

The flags fluttered on their masts, and water-skiers plowed through the waves beyond the shoreside gathering. J. Eisley had arrived and was actively campaigning, but at least he seemed contained to a corner of the crowd with some of his supporters.

As their group was finishing ice cream, Clifton offered rounds of boat rides. Riley and Max fell off their chairs shouting excitedly, and Van and Amy guided them behind Clifton and Rose to the marina dock where he'd moved the boat from Tea for Two's dock.

Jan, Elaine, Bob, and Nathan settled back to visit with each other and other neighbors at nearby tables. The sun was dipping lower in the sky when Elaine looked toward the street and spotted Lila Tate talking with Allie McCall.

Jan was talking with Priscilla Gates, but Elaine got her attention and motioned to Lila and Allie. Priscilla told Jan she'd catch up with her later and moved off to talk to someone else.

Elaine had seen Lila and Allie from a distance throughout the barbecue, but never together until now. Lila had eaten with Ray and stopped by the table to say hello to the Tea for Two group and their friends, but she hadn't lingered.

Allie had been with a small group of girlfriends, but Elaine didn't see them with her now, and it seemed odd that Lila and Allie were standing outside the crowd, as if they wanted privacy.

Jan set her ice cream spoon on her empty plate. "That girl sure makes a lot of friends."

"Which one?"

"Allie."

They watched together until Ray walked up and whispered in Lila's ear, and then they said good-bye and moved off in different directions, the Tates toward the water and Allie to her friends.

"We should have brought her bracelet," Jan said.

"Spying again?"

Elaine and Jan turned back to Nathan and Bob, who were both smirking.

"Just more weird stuff happening around here." Jan adjusted her glasses and smiled coyly at Bob. "Actually, I'm looking forward to a boat ride." The Youngs and Amy's crew made it back to the table, all with boater's hair. The boys plunked down on the bench and asked for more ice cream, and Clifton invited Jan, Elaine, Bob, and Nathan out next.

The boat wasn't new, but Clifton had kept it very clean. Wood-grain finishes complemented the white upholstery. Rose sat up in the bow with her father, Elaine and Nathan took seats in the middle, and Jan and Bob sat in the stern.

The outboard motor roared to life, and Clifton skillfully guided the craft out of the no-wake zone before increasing the speed. The bow tilted up until they planed out, and Elaine raised her face to the rush of fresh lake air. As Clifton steered them around the lake, each of them pointed out different landmarks.

Elaine and Jan snapped pictures with their phones of the other passengers, the back of the tearoom, the marina, the crowd at the Grill, and the Young house across the lake.

Elaine reached over and caught the bubbly spray, cool on her hand. She had to shout over the engine when she told the others she wanted to water-ski sometime. Jan didn't look too sure about that plan, but Nathan and Bob seemed impressed.

Old, Miss Allie McCall? Elaine thought to herself. She'd spent countless hours on this lake growing up and was sure waterskiing would be like riding a bike.

A little while later, Clifton turned back to the marina and moored the craft. The group returned to the seating area and saw Jack Weston and Chuck Yeaton at their table. The two men struck up a conversation with Clifton. Amy and Van were helping their boys to s'mores from a server, a tow-haired boy about fifteen, who asked if anyone else wanted some. Nathan took one, while Elaine took a couple of pictures of Max and Riley with sticky marshmallow-chocolate smiles. "Mom and Dad ought to have fun getting that off."

Van chortled. "We were just deciding whether to dunk them in the lake now or wait and toss them in the bathtub at home."

"Not sure our van can handle their yumminess," Amy added.

"It's all good," Elaine reassured them, though she was glad she wouldn't be the one to clean them up. "They'll be wiping their own faces before you know it."

Amy dipped a napkin in her water cup and attempted to wipe a dollop of chocolate from Riley's face. He grimaced and twisted away from her. "I guess it's the lake," she laughed.

Van nodded a challenge to his boys. "Race you!" All three took off running, with Amy following, toward the water.

AFTER THE RIDE, Jan had accepted Bob's hand getting out of the boat and walked with him to the table, where Max and Riley were getting sticky with s'mores. It had been a near-perfect night with her family and friends. The barbecue was a wonderful diversion after a hectic week.

She enjoyed seeing Bob and her family interact. He fit in fine, joked with Van and treated the boys like big kids, somehow understanding they wouldn't tolerate being treated like preschoolers.

Although she was preoccupied with her group, she tried to pay attention to the circles around her. After Elaine had pointed out Lila and Allie talking together, she kept one eye on the lookout for them.

Eventually she spotted Allie near the band during a short break. Since the musicians were set up next to the dessert tables, Jan asked Bob if he'd like anything sweet and then made her way toward Allie, who looked as if she was deciding whether to indulge in something.

"Go on! You're young," Jan said as she came up next to the young woman.

Allie turned, looking surprised before a smile took over her face. "Jan, right?"

Jan nodded and put two s'mores on a paper plate. "Having fun?" She studied Allie's expression.

"So much fun! I'm glad I didn't have to work late." Allie broke her s'more in two and watched the marshmallow stretch like a rope bridge over a chasm. She managed to get it all back together and then took a bite.

"Have you lived here long, Allie? With the Youngs?" Jan made sure she sounded casual.

Allie worked around graham cracker and goo. "'Bout a month. I grew up in Augusta, so I'm still meeting people." She smiled somehow.

"You seem to make friends easily." Jan flashed a bright smile.

"I like people a lot," Allie said. "I think that's what makes me a good hairdresser."

"That makes sense," Jan said. "Speaking of friends, you know Lila Tate, right?"

For a split second, Allie paused her chewing, then smiled. "I do," she said casually. "Why?"

"Oh, I just saw you chatting with her. She's been in the tearoom, so we've talked some here and there. She's writing a story about our business," Jan said. "We're really excited."

Allie nodded again. But she glanced around before putting on a carefree air. "She was a client this week. She wanted a summery cut...So that's how we met."

Jan looked directly at Allie, fine with making the girl squirm a little. Allie was not telling the whole truth. She nodded and let her gaze linger until Allie looked uncomfortable. After a few moments, Allie excused herself quietly and disappeared into the crowd.

Jan took the plate of s'mores back to the table, where Amy and Van were waiting to say good-bye.

"See you later, Grandma," Riley said. Both boys had wet hair, and Max was rubbing his eyes.

Jan smiled at her daughter. "Not sure these two will make it home awake."

Amy and Van hugged her and left with their kids.

The sunlight was fading quickly, and the crowd was thinning. The waitstaff was lighting tiki torches, which gave the setting a luau ambience. The band even changed up their music to something quieter for those who stayed after dark.

Jan was enjoying the night and didn't feel like hurrying home. Rose was talking with some other friends, and Nathan and Clifton offered to replenish their drinks, so Jan sat with Elaine and Bob and listened to the music.

Before long, Elaine and Bob were talking about waterskiing, and Jan's eyes began to scan the crowd. Now and then a neighbor would wave, and she'd wave back. And then she saw Lila and Ray join some other vacationing couples at a nearby table. The Tates seemed nice enough. They certainly seemed to get along with whomever they met. However, she couldn't see anything different about Lila's hair, whatever Allie meant by a summery style.

Ray straddled the bench next to Lila, and every now and then they whispered to each other. Ignoring the feeling that she was being nosy, Jan peeked at them over her water cup. It looked like they were arguing quietly.

When Lila stood to go, Ray looked at her in frustration but got up and said good-bye to the other couples. Jan turned her attention back to her own table as Nathan and Clifton were returning with the drinks.

Eventually, Jan's group dispersed. Clifton and Rose went toward the marina to drive the boat home, and Bob walked Jan and Elaine down the street to their doorstep. Elaine said good night and went inside, turning the porch light on before she closed the door.

Bob led Jan to the rocking chairs in the shadows away from the door, and they swayed gently in the comfortable air and talked while june bugs found the light. Tree frogs croaked nearby, and time passed quickly. Jan couldn't get over how easy it was to talk to Bob. He could talk enough for both of them but never overwhelmed her with words. And she never felt pressured to keep up the conversation because he seemed to appreciate comfortable silences as much as she did.

He told her more about his law practice; his wife, who died four years earlier; and their twenty-seven-year-old daughter, Susie, in Portland. Jan opened up about Peter and raising three children and now enjoying grandchildren.

He looked thoughtfully across Main Street. "I'd like grandkids someday." He looked at her. "I like yours."

Jan felt shyness wash over her, but it didn't keep her from enjoying the look on Bob's face. "I can tell they like you too." He smiled and she smiled, and something about the moment again felt right, like their paths were meant to cross at this point in their lives. She wondered if he felt anything like that and was fairly sure he wouldn't be sitting next to her if he didn't.

His expression grew more deliberate, and her cautious side kicked in and told her she wasn't quite ready for whatever he might say next. She looked away with a little smile that fell almost immediately when she saw a dark figure walking east past the tearoom on the other side of Main Street. His head was down, but she could tell it was Thomas Spence.

She hadn't seen him all evening, but suddenly there he was walking down the street across from her home. There was nothing casual about his pace either. He was going somewhere—or away from somewhere—with purpose.

Jan whispered to Bob, and they watched him get into a dark sedan down Main Street. Bob reached for his keys, and they jogged down the steps to the Acura. Thomas Spence had a head start, and his car was disappearing into the night as Bob shifted to Reverse and then Drive and pushed hard on the accelerator.

Streetlights shone halos on to the blacktop as the Acura zipped down the road after the sedan's taillights. Jan's blood pumped, and she couldn't suppress a giggle: she was really doing this.

Bob kept his focus ahead, but a smirk played at his mouth. "Be serious. We're after a bad guy."

"I am serious. This isn't my first chase."

He guffawed. "Oh-ho, you're an old hand, huh? Good to know what I'm getting into."

"Keep your eyes on the road." If only he knew! She could see Elaine pumped up for this, but her? Still, Jan had to admit she kind of liked it.

The sedan turned a corner, and by the time Bob made the same turn they'd lost it. They drove around another few minutes but didn't catch sight of the car.

Jan's heart sank. "He definitely wasn't headed toward Waterville. Where could he have gone?"

CHAPTER SEVENTEEN

By eight thirty on Saturday morning, Elaine had already dusted the house and was sorting more donations in the dining room, trying to eke out space for new additions to the piles.

The town had been generous all week, and this was only the second day of the holiday weekend. To Elaine's thinking, the crowds in town had at least doubled, if not tripled, yesterday with the start of the sidewalk sales and farmers' market. She expected today to be even busier with people off work for the weekend and with Teas around the World that afternoon. Jan was at her usual post in the kitchen, humming while she baked special pastries for the event.

There was no story from River in the morning paper, so Elaine figured he must still be gathering info for it.

As she moved crinkly plastic grocery bags and hefted boxes into more orderly positions on the dining table and floor, she caught snatches of the morning news from a Waterville station on the small television in the office across the hall. The anchor was giving an update on the holiday festivities in the local towns, including the Lancaster barbecue.

Elaine set down a carton of peanut butter in jars and met Jan in the office doorway. They watched the rest of the story together.

The camera showed boats lined up in marina slips and then cut to a clip of party-supply company employees dismantling tables and cleaning up outside the Grill. Next, the scene cut to the barbecue, and Elaine saw a couple of shots of their group, including one of the twins and Van jumping into the lake.

Then the next picture surprised both of them.

"Did you see that?" Jan sounded as shocked as Elaine felt.

Elaine grabbed the remote and reversed the story a few seconds. The image blipped, and then once more the face of their mystery man filled the screen for an instant. Thomas Spence's green eyes looked straight at the camera from where he stood behind the Grill, and then he turned quickly and walked out of the shot.

Jan had told Elaine about her adventure with Bob chasing the sedan. "Did you see him there?"

Elaine shook her head.

Jan reached for her phone on the desk and flipped through the pictures she'd taken during the evening. "I don't see him in any of these."

Elaine looked over her shoulder through most of the pictures and then checked her own phone. Nothing caught her eye, but Jan stopped her as she came to the ones taken from the boat.

"Wait. Go back a couple. Yes, there."

The Youngs' home looked lovely from the water, but Elaine didn't notice anything unusual.

The next second Jan's breath caught and she pointed to a spot on the picture. "Make that bigger, will you?"

Elaine stretched the photo, and Jan pointed again. "It's a car up on the road by their house."

Elaine saw Allie's yellow Beetle in the driveway, and sure enough, a dark sedan was sitting on the road.

"He was there." Jan gestured urgently at the phone. "Thomas Spence. That looks just like his car."

"It could be." Elaine tried to stay logical. "But it's pretty generic looking. There're probably dozens of dark sedans in town right now."

Jan pushed up her glasses and frowned at the photo. "Yeah. But that doesn't change the fact that he was driving one of them last night. And you saw him talking to Allie. And her car is there in the driveway."

"You could be right. I didn't see her for a while. Maybe she left to meet him and came back."

Jan was looking again through her own pictures when the door to the back porch clanged shut, and Rose entered the kitchen. She dropped her purse on the table and sank on to a chair.

"What a night," she groaned.

The cousins looked up from their phones.

"After you left, Dad couldn't start the boat because it was out of gas."

Elaine carried her phone to the table and sat down across from Rose. Jan sat in another chair.

"He didn't realize he'd used that much gas taking all of us for rides, but I guess he did. He was embarrassed, but I told him he just had too much on his mind."

"How'd you get home?" Jan wanted to know.

"Tag brought us a gas can. It didn't take long, but then before we could leave Allie called from the house."

Jan and Elaine exchanged looks but didn't interrupt Rose's story to show her the picture.

"She heard some sounds outside and was afraid someone was on the property again."

"Oh!" Elaine felt a look of concern cross her face.

"Dad called Arnie Sheffield, and he met us at the house. We didn't see anything, but Allie was really shaken. She said she was in her apartment when she heard a rattling sound, like a door being shaken, and she saw a flashlight beam near our house. She turned on the outside light of the garage but didn't go outside. A minute later a boat started by our dock and sped off."

"Did Arnie find any clues?"

"The back screen door was bent, and the screen was torn, but that's it. No fingerprints or footprints."

Jan told Rose about seeing Thomas Spence heading out of Lancaster on Main Street. Elaine showed her the picture of the car near their house. Rose grimaced but agreed to call Arnie again and fill him in. Elaine would text the picture to him.

Jan went to fill three cups of iced tea from the gallons she'd made to serve outside. "We saw his picture on the news this morning too. He was at the barbecue when it was still light out."

A possibility occurred to Elaine. "Rose, you said your dad was surprised he'd used so much gas."

"He was shocked. He never runs out, and he filled it up beforehand. I can tell you're thinking something."

"I'm wondering if the intruder could have emptied the tank to keep you away from the house longer."

"When you talk to Arnie, have him dust the boat for fingerprints," Jan suggested.

"Thomas Spence was leaving from the marina at the same time you were discovering the boat wouldn't start? What do you think the chances are he's not in pharmaceutical sales?" It was too bad Jan and Bob hadn't gotten a license plate off the car they tailed last night, but Elaine could hardly fault them. She was actually very impressed.

Rose said she was relieved about one thing. "I almost forgot to lock the doors before leaving yesterday. I'm still only about fifty percent consistent about that. But I remembered and went back yesterday morning."

"How about getting an alarm?" Elaine asked.

"Dad added that to his to-do list."

The morning was moving along. Elaine didn't want to cut short the conversation, for Rose's sake, but they had a lot on their plates for the next few hours. They hurried with the outside display and had things up and running by nine o'clock.

Around ten o'clock, Lydia Pierce pulled up in her car. Elaine and Rose had been monitoring the sales outside when she arrived, and Elaine was surprised that Rose seemed to be expecting Lydia.

A smile lit Rose's face as she hurried to help pull out three garment bags from the trunk. Elaine couldn't imagine what donations would fit in those bags, but Lydia and Rose unzipped them to reveal three new costumes for the afternoon tea.

"How gorgeous!" Elaine couldn't help gushing. There was one in a traditional style from Spain. It was an asymmetrical dress in red and black, with stacked layers of ruffles on the skirt and a scarlet-red headpiece. Another from Mexico had a white, short-sleeved blousy top, yards of a swirling skirt in vibrant purple, yellow, and green, and a coordinating head-band of large roses.

Elaine thought the third costume looked Scandinavian. It had a full black skirt with a waist-high pinafore the color of goldenrod. The bodice had long white sleeves and a fitted red vest with goldenrod-and-black-flowered embroidery. That one came with a white cap that reminded Elaine of a Pilgrim hat. "They're beautiful! And they should work perfectly with today's teas. Rose, did you have something to do with this?"

Obviously she had, the way Rose and Lydia were grinning. "None of us wanted to spend money on another set of costumes, but I thought they added so much last Saturday. And then it occurred to me that the Old Grange might have some things stashed away in their wardrobe department."

Lydia tipped her head charmingly. "And we did."

Elaine thanked both of them and said Jan would be excited to see the surprises. She stayed by the tables while Lydia and Rose took the costumes up to the house.

At noon she posted a new sign on the easel, inviting people to the second Teas around the World at two o'clock. They changed into their borrowed international dresses while the town was sequestered other places for lunch. Jan wore the Mexican costume, Rose the Spanish one, and Elaine the Scandinavian dress. Rose added her mother's white lace shoulder scarf, which looked stunning against the red and black fabric.

From one to two o'clock they were very busy with shoppers in search of desserts. People were stocking up because Tea for Two would not be open on Sunday, and the partygoers didn't want to run out of sweets before Monday.

Customers arrived in droves at two. Seating ran short in both tearooms, so some of the guests helped them pull tables and chairs from the porch into the entry hall to seat those who'd been standing. Conversations filled the cheery space, and the warmth of the woodwork and coziness of the tables and chairs, the fireplace, and the whole setting reminded Elaine for the umpteenth time why she was glad she'd come back to Chickadee Lake.

Elaine, Jan, and Rose took turns introducing a spicy cinnamon chocolate tea from Mexico, a traditional English tea, and a Spanish tea called Maté or yerba maté, traditionally served from a gourd. Their final tea and a special dessert took their guests to Scandinavia.

Elaine explained that the Soderblandning from Sweden was typically a base of black tea infused with fruits like orange rind and florals such as blue petals from cornflower or yellow ones from marigolds. The tea was also popular in Japan, which seemed a more obvious source for such an exotic flavor.

To accompany that tea, Jan and Rose had baked several batches of *kringlas*, a Norwegian cookie with a cakelike consistency and a figure-eight shape that tasted subtly of cardamom, an uncommon spice.

As she described the cookies to the crowd, Elaine couldn't help but think of Clifton's tie tack and the pendant Rose described from her childhood, with their figure-eight detail. Jan and Rose had each taken a cart to a parlor to pass out the kringlas.

Elaine saw many people back again after last week, as well as several who'd heard the rave reviews. The kringlas went fast, and Elaine was glad she'd saved one for herself back in the kitchen. They had an unusual flavor, but one she'd come to love.

She kept a lookout for Thomas Spence but wasn't surprised he didn't show up. She'd seated Mark and Bristol Payson in the east parlor at a table with Pastor Mike and Sarah. And Will and Pearl Trexler had come in with Dr. Tyson and Claudia. Macy Atherton came in to see what the special baked goods were and bought two dozen kringlas, but she didn't stay.

Lila Tate was there without Ray and was sitting at a west parlor table with three women who'd been with their husbands and the Tates at the barbecue. On a trip to that parlor, Elaine saw Lila comment to Rose about her shoulder scarf, and Rose showed Lila the ends of it that had hearts and initials woven into the lace.

Elaine fetched Lila's bracelet from the kitchen and went to stand next to Rose. Lila said a friendly hello and introduced the other women at her table. The opportunity for Elaine to ask Lila a question came up when one of her friends commented about the food at the barbecue.

"Wasn't that a fun night?" Elaine laced her words with enthusiasm. They all nodded. "I couldn't believe how many people showed up. It's amazing how easy it is to meet people around here." She rested a hand on Lila's shoulder. "I noticed you talking with Allie McCall."

Lila's smile was perky and she nodded.

Elaine hoped Rose would follow her lead. To Lila she said, "Did you know Allie rents a room from Rose and her father? And all this time you've known both Rose and Allie. Small world, right?"

Lila nodded again but said nothing.

"How did you meet our friend, Allie?" Elaine handed her the bracelet, and Lila looked surprised.

"Where'd you find this?"

Elaine explained that it must have fallen off when she and Ray had stopped by. "So you met Allie where?"

Lila looked like she was having trouble jumping from one topic to the next. She didn't answer while she dropped the antique bracelet into a pocket of her purse. "I met her just yesterday, actually. We were both looking at the same swim cover-up on a sidewalk rack, and we got to talking, and yeah...she's sweet."

Elaine felt Rose stiffen next to her and was glad she had the sense not to say anything.

Lila smiled up at them. "Let's talk lace sometime soon, okay? If you all have time for that and for a few more questions for my story, my schedule's flexible."

Elaine said she'd talk with Jan and let Lila know what day and time they came up with. She asked the women if they needed anything and returned with Rose to the counter.

"That was interesting," Rose said under her breath. "My vote's still on Allie as the liar."

"Maybe one of them got their story mixed up. Maybe they met at the salon and then again at the sidewalk sale."

Rose made a face. "Just when I was feeling concerned for Allie."

Overall, the tea was another success, and everyone seemed to have a good time. But Elaine was tired by the time the last people finished paying and left. Rose and Jan were passing the counter, pushing teacarts loaded with dishes and centerpiece candles, when Elaine's relief was squashed by River White coming through the door.

He must have seen their antagonistic looks, because he entered with his hands raised and his opening words already on his tongue. "I'll be just a minute, ladies. I know you're probably ready to head home, Ms. Young." He ignored Elaine as she approached to show him the door he'd just come through.

"I hear you had some excitement at your place last night."

Rose stared at him, looking incredulous.

"I was sorry to hear about it, but I'd like to get the details from you so I can make the public aware of a prowler in the area. I want to get the facts right for tomorrow's paper."

Elaine spoke firmly. "We'd like to close up, River."

The light through the front windows shone on his tawny head. "I was also really hoping you'd reconsider talking with me about your mother. I can't get your dad to call me back."

Instead of answering, Rose steered him out the door and practically growled in frustration as he walked down the porch steps, looking over his shoulder to add, "Give me a call."

CHAPTER EIGHTEEN

It was six thirty on Sunday morning, and Brian and Van had come over early, before church, to get started on fixing the office walls. Jan had treated them to breakfast, and she and Elaine were helping with some of the less stubborn sections while the men worked to remove the remaining sheets of wallpaper and the tough old glue.

"So that's the stovepipe hole where someone dropped your sapphire, huh?" Brian was on a ladder, pointing high on the wall shared by the office and the kitchen.

"That's it. Of course, the flue cover covered it up," Jan explained.

"Well, it's about to be unveiled again," Van said amiably.

It was a tedious job removing the paper, but Jan was happy to get some extra time with Brian and her jokester son-in-law. Together they were making progress, and Brian said he hoped to have all the paper down and the glue cleaned from two walls before church.

Elaine stood nearby with a scraper in her hand. "Do you think Clifton and Rose saw the paper yet?" she asked Jan.

"Probably." Using another scraper, Jan gently rubbed at the wall.

The cousins had already read the *Penzance Courier* that had been delivered to the house in the dark hours of the morning. River White's piece focused on Clifton Young and included details of his personal and professional background, including a comment about Aliza's death and the fact that neither Clifton nor Rose had been willing to comment about their family life.

River also mentioned Friday night's attempted break-in, with a quote from Deputy Sheffield that his department was still looking for clues to the intruder.

The article was pretty much what Jan had expected but it still felt a little jolting to see in print.

"It doesn't say anything terrible about them..." Elaine's voice trailed off with a hint of hope.

"No, but it doesn't put Clifton in a great light either," Jan picked up. "He came off sounding kind of secretive, like he has something to hide."

It was true. While the article presented facts, the tone hinted of mystery and a less-than-open attitude from Clifton toward the people he was trying to convince to elect him.

"I'm guessing there'll be a story soon about J. Eisley, and it'll leave the better impression in readers' minds," Jan mused.

"You want to look at those pictures I pulled up?" Elaine changed the subject and motioned to the laptop on the desk. The site she'd found showed a number of old flue covers that homeowners had used to cover holes where stovepipes had once connected to the chimney behind a wall. All of them looked to be a few inches in diameter, like the one Jan was uncovering. Some were flat like theirs. Others were convex or scalloped. Some of them were quite decorative, with pictures of flowers, children, or landscapes.

Elaine and the men stared upward at the wall. "What do you guess ours looks like?"

"I'm sort of looking forward to seeing it," Jan replied.

"Maybe our kids really did do you a favor?"

Brian gave Van a wry smile at his question.

They reached their goal of having two walls prepped for paint, and it was time to take a break. After they cleaned up and the men went home, Jan and Elaine went upstairs to get ready for church.

A while later, they slipped into a pew next to Rose and Clifton. Afterward, when everyone was heading out of the sanctuary, Jan met up with Bob, and they wound up in a huddle in the lobby with Elaine, Nathan, and the two Youngs. Clifton said they'd seen the paper. He had talked again with Arnie Sheffield, and Arnie told him that no prints they'd lifted from the boat or inside the house had pulled up any matches on their databases.

Arnie had talked with Allie, too, and within minutes after he drove away, Allie knocked on the front door of the main house. She was upset that her nosiness had made her a person the sheriff's deputy would question, but Arnie hadn't learned anything from her that warranted more than a stern lecture. With tears that seemed genuine, Allie had apologized for anything she'd done to abuse their trust.

Clifton said it all sounded fine, but he still thought Allie wasn't being entirely honest or forthright. He slapped his palm with his church program as he addressed Jan and Elaine. "Would one of you mind contacting Candace Huang please? I'd like to talk with her today if she can meet."

Jan agreed to set it up.

"We're getting an alarm system installed this afternoon," Rose told them, tucking her hand in her dad's crooked arm.

After lunch Jan found Candace's number and placed the call. When Candace's recorded greeting came on, she left a message asking the reporter to contact her since Clifton was hoping to give Candace his exclusive reply to River White's article. She ended her message and hoped Candace would get back to her soon.

Some of the shops continued their sales on Sunday afternoon, but Jan and Elaine had agreed early on to stick with a day of rest. Jan was glad they'd opted for R & R time even without knowing how much they'd need it. She was antsy, waiting to hear back from Candace, so she spent an hour cleaning bathrooms, sweeping, and washing her Camry while Elaine washed her Malibu. The spray felt good under the warm sun. Then they took a stroll down Main Street to see what the sidewalk sales offered.

They passed the marina, where the theater troupe was finishing a scene from a stage version of Truman Capote's novella *Breakfast at Tiffany's*. They clapped and waved to Lydia Pierce and Diane Blanchett, who were in simple costumes.

The street was crowded, and Jan kept a lookout for Thomas Spence but didn't see him. They decided not to spend a lot of time browsing and kept their shopping brief. Outside Sugar Plum, she found Christmas ornaments for each of her grandkids. For Jared, Elaine bought a chess set Dutch Bigalow had made, which she had seen earlier at Gift Me.

They decided they'd had enough of those crowds and meandered to the farmers' market up Pine Ridge Road next to the Hearthside.

"Happy Sunday, Jan and Elaine!" Annie Richardson called from behind a table lined with buckets of wrapped cheese wedges and bottles of chocolate milk on ice. They bought a wedge of Parmigiano-Reggiano and a block of Havarti with dill.

Elaine also bought a pint of chocolate milk. She popped the top off and elbowed Jan. Annie's sixteen-year-old daughter, Dori, was coming up to the booth with two of her friends, and beyond her Lila and Ray Tate were talking to Dr. Tyson and Claudia at their orchard booth. Jan noticed both Tates were more tanned after a few days outside.

Lila turned just then and saw Jan and Elaine looking at her. "Hey there," she said cheerfully. Ray nodded a greeting.

"Hi, Lila. Claudia, Dr. Tyson."

"I was just telling Mrs. McInnis that Ray and I are looking at lake property this week."

"You mentioned that once before. A vacation place?" Elaine asked.

Ray shifted the paper sack in his arms. "Or more." His voice was lower than Jan had imagined, and she was surprised to realize it was the first she'd heard him speak, at least more than single syllables.

"So you're thinking of moving here?" Jan was surprised by that as well. She hadn't pegged the Tates for year-round small-towners.

But Lila was bubbly. "My aunt used to talk about opening a gourmet kitchen store. She never was able to, and Ray got the idea that it might be perfect here. I could run it and write on the side." She shrugged. "You know, feed the town and my creative juices. You could get specialty spices and cooking gadgets there, Jan."

Jan actually thought that was a fantastic idea. "We could send customers each other's way." Between the magazine story and a specialty store bringing revenue into town, these Tates were turning out to be a treasure trove of possibilities, even with their quirks.

Lila's ideas kept flowing out. "I'd be willing to set up a table so you could sell your pastries there. I might even plant some berry bushes and resurrect my aunt's recipes for currant bread and raspberry cordial and sell those too. She grew those bushes, and I loved eating right off them in the summer."

Jan was about to answer, but Lila suddenly wrinkled her nose and looked guilty. "Which reminds me, I haven't wanted to butt in when you've been so busy, but I really do want to talk more about the tearoom and get another look at that tablecloth. Tomorrow's the holiday. Why don't we wait until later this week to get together?"

"That all sounds great, Lila. I'm excited to see what comes of your ideas."

After the couple walked away, Dr. Tyson blew out his cheeks. "She's a talker, that one."

"She's as chatty as he is mellow," Elaine added.

But Claudia was shaking her head. "The store sounds fine, but she needs to brush up on her Maine facts. She won't be growing currants for that bread of hers. There're a lot of bans on them."

Jan and Elaine waited for Claudia to explain.

"Currants spread white pine blister. Most areas of the state don't allow growing them, mainly the black ones but some red varieties too. Not sure how her aunt got away with it, but maybe the laws weren't as strict back then."

Jan bought a bushel of peaches brought in from Georgia with thoughts of making a pie, and they both tasted samples of blueberry cobbler Claudia had set out in mini cups.

Her phone rang as they were walking back to the house. It was Candace Huang returning her call. After a quick explanation, Jan had Candace on board to talk with the Youngs at six o'clock that evening at the tearoom. Jan called Rose next, and they agreed on the time. Clifton offered to pay for pizza delivery for supper, and Jan was relieved to have that settled.

As they reached the porch steps and were talking about relaxing upstairs with a movie, Jan got a different idea.

"What would you say to a field trip to Waterville? Check out some hotels to see if we can find the one where Thomas Spence is staying?"

Elaine liked that idea and offered to drive.

They put away their purchases and were soon on the road toward Waterville. Jan checked her phone for a list of hotels in town and found several. None were fancy, and she checked off the lower-end ones. Thomas Spence didn't seem the cheap type. She chose three middle-range ones and read their names to Elaine.

"We're assuming he told Bianca the truth. He might not really be staying in Waterville at all," Elaine pointed out.

"I know. When Bob and I followed him, he wasn't going in this direction. But we have to start somewhere, and this is the only lead we have."

"I think we need to offer to help Rose find that brooch. That appears to be the thing that somebody else wants to find."

Jan agreed, and they were still talking about it when they drove into town and the first of the hotels came into view.

They parked and approached a tall woman in a hotel blazer at the front desk. The lobby had the typical hotel smell of air fresheners, laundry detergent, and pool chemicals. A handful of people lounged on chairs and couches in an open area nearby but didn't look up from their newspapers and electronic devices.

"Do you have a reservation?" the desk clerk asked, pleasantly businesslike.

Elaine said no and asked if Thomas Spence was staying there.

As Jan expected, the woman said it was hotel policy not to give out information about their guests. But Jan described what he looked like anyway and asked if there was anyone staying there with his description.

This time the clerk said no dismissively, and Jan and Elaine turned around and left.

"So which one next?" Jan stuck a piece of gum in her mouth and offered one to Elaine. "*Hmm.* How about that one?" She pointed down the road.

They went through the same routine at the desk and were walking out the door when a middle-aged woman in a denim skirt and comfortable shoes stopped them. "I don't want to interfere, but I think I might be staying down the hall from your friend."

CHAPTER NINETEEN

I'm Nancy." She held out a hand and they each shook it.

Then she launched into why she was in town, that she was visiting her late husband's sick mother, and was about to give them her detailed recipe for cheesy tuna casserole when Elaine put a friendly hand on the woman's arm.

"I'm sure it's delicious. Have you talked with him?"

The woman looked befuddled.

"The man down the hall. Might be the one we're looking for?"

A tender look filled the woman's face. "Oh yes. He's not much for chitchat, but we talked on the elevator, and he said his name is Thomas. His hair is the loveliest shade of silver."

"Sounds like our friend," Jan said, with a mischievous glance at Elaine.

"He has an aunt in town who's also sick. That's why he's here. He came all the way from Atlanta."

Elaine didn't want to be rude but wanted to cut to the chase. "Did you happen to see him carry a briefcase or a sample kit, like a pharmaceutical salesman would have?"

"No." Her dishwater-gray roots peeked out as she shook her head. "Nope. He said he isn't working while he's here. That's about all he would say. But I told him it was nice to know someone on my floor. I get a little nervous staying by myself in hotels."

They thanked the woman, wished her a good visit with her mother-in-law, then left.

Sitting in the car in the parking lot, they debated how long to stick around for Thomas to come back.

"This might be our only chance to talk to him," Jan said.

So they waited. The minutes ticked by, turning into hours that started to cramp the time they'd need to drive back to the tearoom for Candace's interview with the Youngs.

They stared at the hotel door and willed their mystery man to show up. They were both sure now that he wasn't a salesman, and they figured a sick relative wasn't the reason he was visiting the area either.

At twenty minutes after five, they gave up and Elaine turned the car toward home.

JAN OPENED THE back porch door for Clifton and Rose while Elaine walked up front to let Candace in. The reporter wore casual shorts and a cotton top and carried a canvas cross-body bag. Glossy black tendrils that had come loose from her bun rested on her olive-skinned cheeks.

After a little discussion, the Youngs chose the east parlor to talk, and Jan and Elaine brought a plate of leftover kringlas and glasses of ice water. Clifton pulled two more chairs around the table.

Candace had brought along a copy of Sunday's *Courier*, and over sausage-and-mushroom pizza and cookies she led the conversation through each point River White had made. She was professional and discreet and had an air of easygoing honesty and impartiality about her.

Clifton and Rose seemed to relax the longer they talked with Candace, who gave them a good hour and a half of her time and showed interest in what they'd learned about Aliza without coming across as though she was after a scoop.

Eventually Clifton and Rose said they'd provided as much information as they could.

"Okay, I just want to recap to make sure I print only what you're ready to share. I know it's sort of unfortunate that you feel pushed into telling people all this before you might like, but I do think this is a good move." She added, "River's a decent guy, even if he comes across overzealous at times."

They agreed she could include the basics of how they became a family, including Aliza's background in East Germany and her escape and custody of Rose, her move to the United States and meeting and marrying Clifton, and his adoption of Rose.

No one saw the need to write anything about the death certificates, Rose's birth parents, US intelligence, the brooch, or the newspaper note. And if readers wondered about the attempted break-in they could chalk it up to an election-related incident. Candace would hint as much, and readers would get over it. She'd also leave it that Rose's birth parents and grandparents were deceased. "There'll be enough other details to steer attention from all that," she promised the Youngs.

She left, assuring them that her editor had agreed to run the story on the front page the next morning, although it probably would be the bottom-fold story since tomorrow was the Fourth of July, and a story centered on the holiday would have priority.

Clifton and Rose left soon after Candace, and Jan and Elaine took cups of tea and sliced peaches up to the sitting room while they watched television.

When Jan offered to take the tray back to the kitchen, Elaine stretched her arms and neck, feeling her muscles loosen. The sun had set, and the sky was giving up its last bits of light. The couch's upholstery felt comfortably scratchy, the lamplight in the sitting room mellow. She had the uncanny feeling something more would happen soon, but for tonight she felt peaceful.

THE NEXT MORNING Elaine watched the sun rise from her perch on the rocky shoreline behind the tearoom. Toward the east, beyond Sylvia's Closet, light was peeking up over the horizon.

Elaine filled her lungs and held her breath as long as she could. Then she let it out in a great, cleansing sigh and picked a dry blade of grass off her black yoga pants. Even when she felt sleepy in the morning, the early start always set her mind right about the day ahead.

She loved that the tearoom kept her connected with people. She loved the activity and the quirks of so many of the town's residents. Most times she even enjoyed the business side of the tearoom, the ordering and bill paying, the invoices and payroll. Organization was good and routine was steadying, especially while she was still figuring out what life should look like after Ben.

She heard the crunch of feet on gravel and turned to see Jan coming to sit by her, also casually dressed for her morning baking. She was managing two full cups and a newspaper under her arm. She dropped the paper on the stones next to Elaine and sat down before handing Elaine one of the teacups.

"Salted caramel?" Elaine guessed after smelling the tea.

"I had a taste for it."

The hot drink warmed Elaine's throat as she picked up the folded paper. The front page was laid out as Candace had said. The bottom half showed a professional headshot of Clifton next to a well-written and honest story that included quotes from him and Rose.

He told the truth, that Aliza had waited to share important details of her past until her final days, and that he and Rose were still adjusting to this new information. He thanked the people of Lancaster for their support and requested privacy and discretion.

Elaine refolded the paper and set it next to her. "I think it sounds great."

Jan held her teacup to her mouth. "She made Clifton seem like himself, a real person again."

Elaine agreed, but the rocks had gotten too hard to sit on any longer, so she told Jan she was heading back to the house to shower and change. "One more day of setup and tear-down and outdoor sales. It's been fun, but I'll be ready to get back to normal."

Jan tented her hand over her eyes to look up at Elaine. "I'm going to finish my tea, but I'll be in to help soon."

Rose arrived in time to help with setup, and then she helped Jan in the kitchen while Elaine unloaded a couple of boxes of flour and sugar that had just been delivered. The UPS truck was rumbling out of the driveway as Elaine overheard Jan give Rose extra tips about a fussy meringue cookie recipe Rose was making.

Elaine carried the flour and sugar into the pantry and then broke down the boxes for recycling before she went to the office to mark the order as received.

With a little time to spare before she needed to cover things outside, Elaine poured herself another cup of tea and offered to help in the kitchen.

"How 'bout dish duty?" Jan asked.

Elaine got to work loading spatulas and measuring cups and spoons into the dishwasher, then plugged the sink and ran warm water from the tap and added a squirt of dish soap to hand wash some things.

She ran her hands through the silky bubbles while she listened to the easy camaraderie of Jan and Rose. She knew Jan was enjoying Rose's growing interest in baking.

"Rose," Elaine ventured, "have you thought much more about the brooch?" She handed the clean mixer bowl to Jan, who was starting on a double batch of spritz cookies.

Rose was putting the meringue cookies in the top wall oven. "Dad and I turned the house inside out again looking for it. Mom couldn't believe after all she and Dagmar had been through and talked about..." She exhaled a tight laugh. "Maybe someday I'll be able to say my *mother* instead of *Dagmar*...Anyway, what I'd give to know if that brooch has been hidden under our noses all this time. Not only because someone else seems to know about it, but because I'm having a hard enough time making sense of all these new things about my mom, and I guess I'm looking for closure wherever I can find it."

Rose had kept her cool amazingly well in the past week, but every now and then her vulnerability showed. She shrugged. "I've tried out the name Tatiana Rose a few times. It still sounds strange, but that was my name. I wish Mom would've talked to me about all this. I know she had good reasons not to. But she was my only connection to my birth mother...and the other people in my family."

"There've got to be ways to find out more about them," Elaine offered.

That seemed to make Rose hopeful. "Dad's words that she *couldn't* tell me, not that she *didn't* tell me, keep running through my head."

"I guess that needs to be your peace right now," Jan replied.

The pastries were about finished, and they'd started to clean up the final round of dirty dishes when the doorbell rang.

It wasn't even eight thirty. "Someone's anxious for an early snack." After a quick check of her hair and lip gloss in the powder room mirror, Elaine walked up front. As she neared the entry, she looked more closely through the door's glass and had to work to keep her jaw from dropping.

Jan and Rose were going to love this, she thought, reaching for the antique doorknob. A few days ago she wasn't sure she could pick him out of a crowd, but now Elaine recognized him immediately.

She swung open the door and looked into the green eyes of Thomas Spence.

CHAPTER TWENTY

He says he's going golfing for the day, but he was hoping he could get some tea and a snack to go," Elaine said in a fervent whisper.

"He's still here? In our house?" Jan asked, appalled. Fear grabbed her until a latent fierceness rose up and squelched it.

They peeked around the kitchen wall. Thomas Spence raised a hand in a stiff salute from the entryway.

"Looks like he hasn't moved."

Rose was wiping her hands on a dish towel with a determined look in her eye. "Let's go meet this guy." She threw the towel on to the counter, resecured her hair in a clip, and then strode out of the kitchen. Jan and Elaine followed.

Jan couldn't believe the man was in her own house, but she didn't have time to wonder about it. Now was her chance to finally find out what he was up to.

"Thanks for opening early for me." He smiled at each of them, which caught Jan off guard. He was more solid-looking up close. He had to be sixtyish, but his arms still had the definition of a man who'd stayed fit all his life.

"I'll pay you extra for the trouble. I'm meeting friends for golf in Waterville in thirty minutes, and I said I'd bring breakfast."

He wore plaid shorts, a red polo shirt, and canvas penny loafers. His gold watch shone on his wrist; his gray hair was trimmed short. His gaze was friendly and direct, without any of the aloofness of Jan's first meeting with him.

He seemed like any other vacationer. She'd prepared herself for a confrontation, but she hadn't expected this mannerly and unassuming man to show up for it.

Jan lowered her eyelids. "You drove here from Waterville for *muffins*, only to drive back for golf?"

Not even a flicker to show that the question had thrown him. In fact, he looked slightly amused, but not in a patronizing way. He actually seemed borderline charming.

Absurd.

"I did," he answered smoothly. No explanation. His green eyes just twinkled. "It doesn't need to be muffins. Two dozen of whatever's easiest to pack would be marvelous."

Then he looked at Rose. "I believe I met your father once," he said, offering his hand.

"Really." The word was laced with skepticism. She stared a moment at their joined hands, the dubious look still on her face. "Jan here tells me you asked about me last Saturday."

Thomas let go and clasped his hands in front of him and admitted that he had. "I don't know that Clifton would remember me, but he and I met at a medical conference a long time ago. I sell pharmaceuticals."

Rose beat Jan to the question. "Are you here on business?"

"I am," he said quietly. His voice was measured, his words deliberate. "But I'm enjoying the area too."

"*Mmm*, yes, lovely place. What did you think of Dr. McInnis's office? Not exactly the Mayo Clinic, but it works for us."

Rose rattled off the words, and Jan almost laughed at her moxie. The woman was on a mission; she was done being messed with. Rose's blue eyes flashed, and a snatch of wheat-colored hair flopped loose from her hair band, giving her a girlish look despite the challenge in her tone and body language.

"I'm planning to stop there tomorrow. The doctor's probably not in today."

"Where is home for you?" As Jan asked the question, she watched Elaine slip away toward the kitchen and hoped she'd return soon so she wouldn't miss this conversation.

"Georgia. An hour south of Atlanta." So that much fit with what Nancy told them.

"You don't have an accent," Jan accused.

"I'm not there much, and I'm originally from Utah."

"You're probably a skier then."

"I've done my fair sh—"

"My cousin's daughter lives in Colorado and loves the skiing, but she raves about the Utah slopes."

"Both places have their perks."

"Is this your first time to Maine?"

"No."

"So how long are you in the area, Mr. Spence?"

His quizzical look halted her rapid-fire questioning. Jan felt her face warm as she realized he hadn't offered his name.

Rose lifted her chin. "We get to know people pretty quickly around here."

A smirk twitched Thomas Spence's mouth. His face bore faint wrinkles, and Jan now noticed that a scar crossed his brow. To her relief, Elaine appeared from the kitchen with two white to-go boxes.

"We'll walk you out," Elaine said, leading the way to the door. "I need to get to the sale tables anyway. You've given us a good start." Elaine's smile was perfectly composed, and her voice matched the smoothness of Thomas Spence's.

Jan pressed a hand to her abdomen. Her insides were still churning.

Thomas Spence's dark sedan was parked in front of Sylvia's Closet next door, even though the spaces were empty in front of the tearoom. He turned to say good-bye to the women and Jan wasn't about to miss her chance.

"Were you near the Youngs' house Friday night?"

He turned back to face her and smiled easily. "I was. I looked up Clifton's address and thought I'd stop by to visit again. But he wasn't home."

"Someone tried to break in our house that night."

He looked seriously at Rose for a moment. "I heard about that. I'm glad they weren't successful. Please say hello to your father for me. I hope everything works out…with the election." He slipped sunglasses on to his face and turned again to go.

He pointed his key fob at his car. The taillights lit up and the locks beeped. He got in and drove off without looking back.

Jan's neck and shoulders felt stiff. She knew her questions made her appear defensive to him, but she didn't care. "He didn't pay for the muffins."

Elaine and Rose burst out laughing, and then Jan was laughing too. "Would one of you please tell me what just happened?" she asked, trying to catch her breath.

"*That* was our dreadful stalker?" Elaine said.

Jan rolled her eyes. "Just because he surprised us by acting nice doesn't mean he's suddenly innocent."

Rose looked more serious. "No, but his story works. Just because he wasn't friendly a week ago doesn't make him guilty of anything, I guess. I'll ask Dad about him, but he's probably right that Dad won't remember him from one conference a long time ago."

Jan smiled reluctantly. "I suppose we did give him the third degree a little. He told Nancy at the hotel that he's visiting a sick relative. I guess that could still be true."

"He didn't seem to mind our questions. And he seemed supportive of Dad. I'll take it."

Jan sighed. "Well, he did forget to pay."

CHAPTER TWENTY-ONE

Thomas Spence weighed on Jan's mind all morning, even though she was plenty occupied keeping the kitchen running and checking on the outside setup, the parlors, and front counter, and then returning to the kitchen for refills of tea and pastries. Today they could really use that additional help they'd talked about hiring.

It was the final day of celebration. Not only was there a steady stream of customers at Tea for Two, but most of them came in lugging shopping bags loaded with finds from the sales around town.

The friendly atmosphere was contagious, and Jan felt energized. Rose split her time inside and out too, manning both inside parlors and the porch tables, while Elaine sold baked goods and iced tea and accepted donations. Elaine wasn't bashful about enlisting help from friends who stopped by and were willing to empty a donation bin in the dining room.

Bob came in around one o'clock and asked Jan if she'd like to sit together for the fireworks that night. She accepted with preoccupied cheeriness, then took him up on his offer to help by sending him to the garage for an old sun umbrella to set up outside so Elaine could have shade. He also boxed up more pastries to go, loaded the dishwasher, washed some dishes by hand, refilled the iced tea urns and lugged them outside for Elaine, and gave Jan's shoulders a few quick squeezes when he caught her rubbing them in the kitchen.

Brian, Paula, and their girls avoided the crowd by coming in through the back porch. The girls were finishing ice cream cones, and they'd been to the farmers' market and filled Jan and Elaine's refrigerator crisper drawers with local produce. Brian worked some more on the office walls. Paula said her family and Amy's would join them for fireworks at dusk, but Tara had plans with friends.

At four thirty, the tearoom was still full, but by five o'clock the parlors had thinned enough that Jan went to lock the front door. Near the front sidewalk, Brian had taken a break from the office walls to help Elaine dismantle everything for the final time.

She unlocked the door again so they could get back in but flipped the Open sign to Closed and checked with Rose to see how far she'd gotten wiping tables. Amy's and Brian's families both came back and helped wash the piles of teacups, saucers, spoons, and other dishes that wouldn't fit in the dishwasher's sixth run of the day.

When everything was back to normal, Jan and Elaine dropped on to kitchen chairs. Rose left with a box of cookies and said she'd be back with her dad for the fireworks later that night. Jan had invited the Youngs to watch the show with them from the backyard.

When Brian and Van offered to foot the bill for takeout from the Grill, Jan was eager to accept. She felt like a mess. Her teal shirt was frosted with flour, which she suspected was in her hair too. A dried egg streak was flaking on her pant leg, the red polish on her right big toe was chipped from a whisk that fell on it, her face was greasy from hours over a mixing bowl, and her bare lips screamed for balm. With twenty minutes or more before Brian and Van returned with supper, she and Elaine begged off to clean up.

When she emerged from her room, refreshed and dressed in jean shorts and a red gingham top, she met Elaine in the upstairs hallway and the grandkids coming back downstairs from the third floor. Elaine had changed into blue shorts and a red-white-and-blue plaid shirt.

On the way down the stairs, Kelly reached for Jan's hand and they walked to the kitchen together. Jan melted at the touch of her granddaughter's warm skin.

Supper was cheery and noisy and filling, and Jan loved every minute. Bob showed up halfway through the meal and soon had a full plate of samples from the others' entrees.

The women ate at the table, while the men and kids stood around the island, talking about boating and fishing and Kelly's recent karate tournament and Avery's upcoming gymnastics meet. By the time Jan's stomach was full of coconut shrimp and sweet potato fries and her emotional tank refilled, she was ready for a fun night of fireworks.

Heading outside with sunscreen and some spray to ward off the Maine mosquitoes, they brought blankets and lawn chairs down to the lower deck.

The sun hung half hidden by trees beyond the marina. "The sun looks like it's not sure whether to set yet," Jan said to Bob.

"Maybe you could reassure it that man-made fireworks can't outdo its brilliance."

With that, the fiery orb seemed to drop a little lower.

The kids ran toward the water to look for crayfish and frogs. Avery called out that she'd seen a turtle, and Max was stopped by his mother's voice right before he plunged into the water after it.

He threw Amy a grumpy look, and the adults couldn't help laughing. Van called all four back to the seating area and surprised them with giant Pixy Stix. When Amy and Paula didn't look thrilled, he waved them off. "It's the Fourth of July!" He raised his fists with a loud *Woo-hoo!* and chased his sons into hysterical giggles around the yard. Jan saw Brian look on with a grin.

Just when she was sure the night couldn't get any better, Bob offered her a seat in one of the chairs he'd brought and sat down next to her.

Dozens of boats bobbed on Chickadee Lake, many strung with Christmas lights. Tiki torches dotted the shore where other groups had gathered.

An evening breeze toyed with Jan's hair. She pushed a curl behind her ear while she glanced sideways and caught Bob looking at her. She smiled back at him and was about to tell him she was happy he was there, when Clifton and Rose appeared from around the side of the house with lawn chairs.

Rose had let her hair down and looked beautiful with it draped around her shoulders. They'd changed into shorts and flag shirts too and made the rounds of greetings before setting up their chairs. With a laugh, Clifton turned down Van's offer of Pixy Stix he'd pulled from his hidden stash.

"How many do you have?" Amy asked her husband.

He shrugged and pulled another one from under his chair for her.

When the sun finally dropped out of sight, Amy and Van and Brian and Paula snuggled up with their kids on the blankets. Darkness finally came, and with it a blast of the national anthem from a large raft on the lake that would be the launching pad for the display. The sky erupted with boom after boom, and Jan was transported back to her childhood when she'd watched this show every summer.

They *ooh'd* and *ahh'd* over each one, and the twins inched closer to their parents' laps as the night crept later past their bedtime. Jan remembered breathing in the pure earthiness of her own young kids after a day of play.

When she sensed Bob looking over at her again, she realized she'd sighed in contentment. The night felt like a link between the past and present, with hints of the future sparking across the sky. She could tell Bob was thinking about what would come next, how they would navigate what was happily developing between them.

She'd let him take his time, trusting his pace in sharing any feelings. She was okay enjoying the moments one by one.

She hadn't always been one to live in the moment and often got caught up in to-do lists and ought-to's. But something about being back in Lancaster with the tearoom and Elaine and her children and grands nearby—and Bob...All of it was telling her to savor each bit of life like a new blend of tea. She hadn't expected this happiness to catch her, but she was glad it had.

She looked around at the people she considered close enough to join her at her home. Clifton and Rose had become dear friends these past days. Even though they did not match biologically, their bond was unmistakable. They were a set.

She thought of Aliza and felt a pang of sadness for all that Aliza had lost but that had burdened her for so long. She must have felt so alone at times, even with a loving husband and child. Jan could imagine Aliza's loneliness might have been compounded by a longing to open up to the people who cared for her the most. But she'd loved them more than herself and she'd done her best to protect them.

Jan thought further back in time to the scenes she'd imagined from the tidbits of information she knew about Aliza when she was Fredda Beck, safe in her parents' home before all the trouble started.

And then with tiny Tatiana in West Germany, as her resources diminished and her fears grew that she wouldn't be able to keep her promise to Dagmar.

No mother could be perfect, but a single day with Rose told so much about the woman who'd invested everything in her. Rose had two mothers, and both had sacrificed themselves to give her life.

Aliza could have returned Tatiana Rose to the Schultzes or found her a different home. And after the government returned the private companies to their original owners, when Rose was still a tiny child, Aliza could have given her up and gone back to reclaim her family's business, her own heritage and livelihood. Her link to her own parents.

But Aliza had chosen Rose. She had loved Rose more than her own life, and Jan believed that Rose had become Aliza's world, along with Clifton.

When things settled down for Rose, Jan would broach those thoughts with her, from a mother's perspective. Rose had been deeply loved by her birth mother *and* her adoptive mother. Not everyone could say that.

Jan felt a bond with Rose too, and although she might not use the word *mentor* herself, she'd heard Elaine comment to that effect about Jan's role in the younger woman's life. It was an honor that made the tearoom even more special.

Jan thought next about the raid on the Beck home, how they must have panicked as Ernst was pulled away from them, and the theft of so many symbols of their life together.

God was there the whole time, and He'd worked out so many details. Jan was confident that He had made sure Fredda and Ane were left with Ernst's tie tack. And by allowing Georg and Rolf Schultz to steal the Becks' matching pendant and the diamond brooch, He created a link to Dagmar Schultz that would bond her and Fredda in a friendship that became like family for both of them, and for Tatiana Rose. It was a link between two families that were Rose's heritage.

The story was difficult and beautiful, the finger of God guiding each step of the way.

But where was the brooch? And who wanted it? With all the detail Dagmar went to in creating a custody document and letting Fredda know she was doing it, with all the time she and Fredda spent together, confiding in each other, Dagmar would have planned the best possible hiding place for the brooch.

She just would have.

Looking at the situation from a mother's perspective, Jan saw young Dagmar covering every detail about her child's future, including how she would provide for Tatiana Rose across the Wall. The brooch that was shared by the Beck and Schultz families could be the tool that would help Dagmar and Fredda rebuild their lives and make a life possible for Tatiana Rose.

Her motherly intuition told Jan that Dagmar had chosen a very special place to hide the brooch, a place no one except Fredda would think to look. For Tatiana Rose's sake, but also because it was rightfully Fredda's since it had become Dagmar's only at a loss to Fredda's family.

Dagmar made sure Fredda had the brooch in her possession in West Germany. And if Fredda brought everything with her to America, then the brooch should still be among Aliza's things...somewhere. It had to be in the Youngs' house.

Somewhere in the distance a siren droned and gradually faded.

The next firework exploded, bringing with it a new thought: one of the photos from Aliza's scrapbook. The close-up of Fredda and her friend, who was surely Dagmar, holding their hair back in the wind—Jan hadn't paid much attention to it, but now, suddenly, it was as if the fireworks were shining on the bracelet around Dagmar's wrist.

In her mind's eye, the bracelet seemed to be moving in the picture, jostling in the wind.

Just like Lila Tate's bracelet with the clasp that kept coming undone...Lila, with her perky nature and watchful eye toward Rose. Who was Lila Tate, really? What were the chances that she and Ray happened to vacation in town the week all the odd events started happening surrounding Aliza's past?

Lila was mixed up about whether her aunt or grandmother was the seamstress, and if she herself had the experience she claimed—enough to open a gourmet kitchen store—she probably would have been more careful not to mistake cornstarch for baking powder. And she claimed her aunt grew currants in Maine, which wasn't even legal. It was entirely possible that both Lila and Allie lied about how they met.

And then there was Lila's interest in the lace. Not many people knew lace-making, but Lila did. She even understood to look for the pictures woven into the pieces.

It made Jan wonder. Those pictures were one of the things that made the lace so special. Perhaps she'd take a look at the tablecloth again. If it was handmade by Aliza, maybe she'd found a way to communicate her heart through those very pictures. Maybe they said something about Aliza they didn't yet know.

A cell phone rang nearby, and Clifton's abrupt movements told Jan it was his. She couldn't hear what he was saying, but suddenly he got up and gestured for Rose to come with him.

As they were running toward their car, Rose called back, "Someone tripped the alarm! The police are on their way to our house."

Jan looked across the lake, but all she saw were lights on boats invisible in the blackness.

When the group arrived at the Youngs' house, two squad cars had already arrived, and Jan leaned forward when she saw an ambulance there too.

They piled out of the Acura and joined Clifton and Rose by the ambulance, where two EMTs were kneeling over someone.

Bob put a hand on her elbow.

Jan's first thought was Allie, and she prayed she was wrong.

Elaine pulled her closer to the injured person. At first she couldn't see anything through the EMTs, but then a flash of an arm told her the victim was too large and muscular to be Allie McCall. Whoever it was had been on the property before Clifton and Bob drove up. If this was the intruder, then how did he end up hurt on the ground?

"More than one person had to have been here," Elaine said in a low voice. "Why would the intruder be lying on the ground?

Rose came to stand by Jan and Elaine. Her hair was tousled around her shoulders.

Bob and Clifton were jogging toward the back of the house, where officers were shining flashlight beams around the yard. A minute later light shined through the windows.

"They're in," Elaine said softly.

Rose wiped her nose and seemed to notice the person on the ground. "Allie?"

Jan reassured her it wasn't Allie McCall. That just left the question hanging: Who *was* it?

Jan hadn't met any of the EMTs in town, but these two—a man and a woman—were helping the person to his feet.

Elaine covered her mouth and Rose stumbled.

"Thomas!" Jan gasped.

Thomas looked a little battered and worn. His right T-shirt sleeve was torn, and a streak of red like blood crossed the front of his shirt. Something didn't look right about his face, and as Jan started forward again she saw a purple bruise staining his left cheek.

As she came up behind an EMT her eyes met Thomas's. He shrugged off the ice pack the EMT had been holding to his head and crossed the last few feet between them. He looked from her to Rose and then at the house and shook his head.

Trooper Benson appeared out of nowhere and looked ready to pounce.

Thomas's mouth narrowed to an angry, thin line, and he winced as if a shot of pain hit him. "I got here as the alarm went off, but they surprised me. I managed a few hits before he nailed me on the side of the head and I went down. I don't know how long I was out, but they've got a good head start. You need to call in an APB on..."

CHAPTER TWENTY-TWO

Ray Tate!" Jan's knee-jerk response came out even before Trooper Benson could speak.

Fireworks exploded overhead and Thomas paused midwince to look at her. Trooper Benson had disbelief in his eyes.

"It was her bracelet"—Jan's words poured out—"and some other things, but her bracelet fell off, and it reminded me of a picture I'd seen in Aliza's scrapbook." She had found it, had it in her possession, but she hadn't really *seen* it until she recalled the bracelet in the photo.

She turned to Rose. "Remember the one of your mother and Dagmar? Dagmar was wearing a dark silver chain bracelet, and it occurred to me on the way here that it looked an awful lot like Lila's."

Trooper Benson looked like he wasn't taking Jan seriously, but Thomas held up a hand to quiet him. It was the same gesture he'd given to Jan the first day in the tearoom. But this time she took it entirely differently and was relieved he wanted to hear her out.

"Call Arnie Sheffield." And then her words started running together again as she explained that Ray and Lila Tate were vacationers who were considering buying a lake home, and Lila said she was writing a story about the tearoom—but who knew now if that was true—and while they seemed friendly enough, Lila was a little extra curious about the lace, and how her story didn't match Allie's about how they met, and on and on.

Thomas cut in, addressing the state trooper. "You need to put out an APB on Ray and Lila Tate." He squinted at his gold wristwatch. "They're driving a black BMW SUV, and they left here approximately thirty-five minutes ago. I didn't see which direction they went because Ray was the one who knocked me out. I got here as they were leaving after setting off the alarm." He nodded to Jan. "Mrs. Blake is right.

"My name is Thomas Spence, retired CIA. We've wasted enough time. You need to make that call *now*."

FORMER CIA AGENT Thomas Spence leaned forward on the sofa with his elbows on his knees, his head in his hands. Elaine wasn't sure how old he was, but right now he looked like he'd earned that retirement he ought to get back to. She'd seen her fair share of spy movies, and now that she knew his identity, he fit the image. She was amazed she hadn't pegged him earlier as some sort of government agent.

It was 12:30 a.m. on July 5 when Elaine handed him a large mug of hot peppermint tea. "Here, take this. It won't fix the pain, but it can't hurt."

She was in her upstairs sitting room with him, Jan, and the Youngs. The house was dark except for the two lamps that glowed softly in the room. Jan sat in Grandma's rocking chair, and Clifton and Rose were sitting in the other chairs. All four of them looked wiped out.

She and Jan and Thomas had stayed late at the Youngs' while they did a preliminary check to see what might be missing. Trooper Benson took down Thomas's and the Youngs' statements, and Jan and Elaine filled in gaps based on all they'd investigated. The APB had been called in, and now it was a waiting game until they heard news about the apprehension of Ray and Lila Tate for assault and various other crimes.

Several rooms had been ransacked, and Rose and Clifton took Jan and Elaine up on the offer of their guest room and sitting-room couch for the night to give the officials more time to dust for fingerprints. They'd go back over later that day to do a more thorough search.

Bob went home from there, and Jan invited the others to the tearoom so they could hear more from Thomas about the mysterious years of Aliza's life that were still such a blank slate to the rest of them. Thomas was a link to her in a way no one else could be.

Elaine had brought tea for the others as well, and she curled up cross-legged on the rug on a big pillow she'd brought from her room.

"Do you think they found the brooch?" Elaine risked asking him.

He shrugged. So he knew about it. Elaine couldn't wait to hear what else he knew.

He rubbed his face, then ran both hands through his disheveled gray hair and looked at Clifton. "I helped your wife come to America. My department had been surveilling Georg and Rolf Schultz for years. There's a lot I'm not free to tell you, but I'll give you what I can.

"You were right to wonder about the Tates. Lila is Georg's great-niece, who's been living in the States for more than twenty years. Their real names are Ray and Sabine Meyer. Apparently she heard stories when she was growing up about Dagmar and Fredda and the lost child Tatiana. She grew up and got married and told Ray all about it, and here we are. I saw Ray let the gas out of your boat at the barbecue, so I drove to your house ahead of them. They're looking for the brooch, and I gave them some space to see how far they planned to go. It's taken them a long time to find you, Rose."

She must have done her research about how to trick Rose, Elaine thought. Saying she was a writer from the magazine was an effective ruse, and Elaine couldn't help feeling disappointed that not only had this woman been out to steal from Rose and Clifton, but also she got Jan and Elaine's hopes up about being featured in a magazine. Of course, that wasn't what was important here, and she'd have to ignore that pang of disappointment for now.

He looked at Rose. "Not being affected by people is part of my job. But you need to know that I've been checking in on you and your mother since I helped bring you to Maine." His features softened. He took a gulp of the scalding tea, making Elaine wince as she imagined the heat burning his throat.

"I met Fredda Beck and you, Tatiana, when I approached her in a park one day. She had no idea I'd been watching you both. Actually, I was watching the Schultz house early on the morning when she left with Dagmar Schultz. I knew about the custody paper Dagmar had drawn up for you, and I made sure the lawyer finished it on time. Once we knew about her plans to cross the Wall, my department put it in motion to approach both Fredda and Dagmar in West Germany. It was my job to monitor the house because we didn't know exactly when it would happen."

He looked at Clifton and then back to Rose. "Long story short, I was in the courtroom and watched her yell to Fredda to 'find it.' After Dagmar's death, Fredda never told me about the brooch, but we knew enough to suspect that was what Dagmar meant."

He took a deep breath and ran a thumb around the rim of his mug. "My job was to keep track of Fredda because she'd lived in Georg Schultz's home, and we still thought she could help us. Rolf had been dead a year and a half or so, but we were always more interested in Georg. Just because the countries were reunited didn't mean men like Georg Schultz were suddenly believers in western democracy. He was on our watch list until the day he died."

Elaine could see fissures in Thomas's façade. A traumatized and lonely young woman with a blonde-headed toddler had gotten to him all those years ago.

It occurred to Elaine that somewhere in the information Thomas just shared was the reality that Rose would have grown up loving Dagmar as her mother, had the escape not happened.

But then again, if Dagmar had been correct about her controlling in-laws, maybe Rose would have lost Dagmar anyway and would have grown up with Georg and Berta Schultz.

Thomas continued. "Fredda agreed almost immediately to go to America. She knew she couldn't make it work in West Germany, and I think she wanted to get as far away as she could from all that had happened to her. It was reassuring to her, the thought of being protected across the ocean by our government. We offered the two of you a new life, and she gave us important information about Georg Schultz."

"Why was he never punished?" Clifton asked.

"He and his wife died in an automobile crash some years after Aliza and Rose were transferred to the US." His expression softened for Rose. "About the move...Aliza picked your new names, and we chose Maine." He rubbed his hand through his hair, making it stick up in places. "It wasn't protocol for me to accompany you here. A home agent could've taken it over while I stayed on the field overseas. But I wanted to make sure you were okay. Aliza got a job in a bookstore and took ESL classes. She wanted to get rid of her accent. I think she was scared of being tracked down, and she was right to fear Georg Schultz. More than once we threw him off your trail."

"So you gave us new birth certificates, American ones," Rose said.

He nodded.

"And you made the two death certificates happen."

He nodded again.

Clifton looked mellow. "You said you've been keeping an eye on Aliza."

Thomas nodded. He really had a kind smile, Elaine thought.

He knew about Aliza and Clifton's wedding and the adoption. And he sent the article to Aliza about the Schultzes' deaths. He knew when Rose graduated from middle school, then high school and college, and when she moved to Portland and back to Lancaster.

Rose looked like she was weighing her comfort level.

"You're wondering if I've been lurking behind trees, aren't you?" he asked her with a smile. "Aliza knew my colleagues in the area would be checking in every now and then without her knowing it. You weren't to be disturbed. After I retired seven years ago, I returned to the States and checked in on you myself a few times."

"So you knew when Mom died."

Again he nodded.

"Soon after her death, I was contacted by a former coworker who's still active. They had a lead on some suspicious movement from Georg's old camp. They were sending someone on the ground here to monitor things this week, but I wanted to do it, so I convinced them to let me back in for this one job."

He took another sip of tea.

"Are there any others...relatives...who might cause trouble?" Rose asked.

"I don't think so. And as far as we're concerned, the brooch belongs to you. Don't ask how, but we tracked down the bill of sale when we needed to know just what was at stake. It proves it originally belonged to Ernst and Ane Beck, your grandparents by adoption."

Elaine's mind went back to the events of the evening, remembering how Allie had shown up as they were walking through Clifton and Rose's house. She panicked and was worried about what had happened. Elaine couldn't imagine it that it had been an act. When Allie heard about the APB on the Tates, she started sobbing and apologizing to Rose and Clifton, admitting she shouldn't have trusted Lila Tate, who had approached her outside A Cut Above as Allie was leaving work one evening.

Being Allie, she was insatiably curious. Lila gave her a cock-eyed story about knowing Aliza from a book group the previous year, when Lila supposedly had visited Chickadee Lake for the entire summer. They'd become friends, and Lila had loaned her valuable brooch to Aliza for an event she was going to with Clifton.

According to Lila, Aliza had forgotten to return the brooch, and a year passed while Lila was back home forgetting to ask Aliza to return it. Now that Aliza had recently died, Lila felt terrible asking Rose or Clifton to look for it, so would Allie accept five hundred dollars to search her landlord's house for it on the sly? Allie said all she'd done was snoop, and yes, she was the one who rolled the tree stump under the window.

A brief lull had fallen when Thomas finished speaking, but Jan broke it. "What were you doing talking with Allie in town? I saw you and wondered what you could be up to."

"Asking what Lila Tate wanted from her," Thomas replied. "Allie's reply was vague enough to arouse even more suspicion." He had warned her to steer clear of the Tates, who'd only lead her into trouble. Allie claimed she had only snuck into the house once.

Earlier that evening Clifton had pulled Trooper Benson aside and told him he didn't want to press charges against Allie. At Rose's suggestion that she stay with a friend, Allie got into her car and drove off.

But now it was time to let everyone finally get some sleep. "Thanks for coming over, Mr. Spence. Here, I'll take your teacup down to the kitchen and walk you out." Jan picked up the others' cups as they stood to bid Thomas farewell, agreeing that they'd be in touch soon.

Fifteen minutes later, Elaine turned off her bedside lamp and reached her toes far under the sheets, enjoying the coolness. Now, if only she could turn off her racing thoughts so easily!

CHAPTER TWENTY-THREE

Jan stepped out of the bathroom and hugged her thick white robe tighter around herself. Although it was midsummer and warm outside, she felt chilled as she got ready for bed.

Her body was tired, but she was sure her brain was even more so. She'd processed so much information in one night—after the physically taxing day of work—that she wasn't sure she'd wake up in time to open the tearoom at ten. She definitely wasn't going to do any early-morning baking. The freezer stock would have to do. Honestly, she'd be okay with a light day and figured it might even happen since so many people had flocked through the town over the past four days.

She flipped off the overhead light, then made her way to her bed by her night-light's glow. She climbed under the sheet and blanket and would have been asleep instantly if it weren't for something that had nagged her subconscious ever since they'd sat down to listen to Thomas's story. It was something she'd thought of earlier in the evening, but for the life of her she couldn't place it now.

She took a deep breath and tried to push away the urge to remember. She turned to her other side and fluffed her pillow before resetting herself. The clock on the bedside table blazed a steady red, reminding her every second that it was 2:02, 2:02, 2:02, 2:03...

Her eyes shot open. Red glowed: 2:34, 2:34, 2:34...She'd fallen into a fitful sleep, only to be wakened suddenly with the realization of what she'd been trying to put her finger on.

Bone tired but wired, she went to her closet, where she'd put the tablecloth on a shelf, and turned that light on too. Sitting on the oak floorboards, she unfolded the fabric and spread it across her blue pajama pants. Inch by inch she studied it. The artistry was decent but not perfect. Her trained eye helped her notice details a novice might miss.

Now her close inspection, even through bloodshot eyes, told her this tablecloth must have been one of Aliza's earlier works. Maybe something Ane Beck had instructed an adolescent Fredda to make for her hope chest. Every stitch in the smaller handkerchiefs and window ornaments had been perfection. This one was special, for sure, but perhaps more so because of its flaws. Granted, this was a much larger piece, but that would only have meant more time, not more difficulty, to a skilled lace maker.

She ran her fingers over each inch, studying it. Her eye caught on something. In the third corner, she found two letters, initials, like an artist's signature. Not the initials she would have expected, but ones that made sense for this piece. The letters were *DS*. Not *FB* as in Fredda Beck. *DS* as in Dagmar Schultz.

In all the time Dagmar and Fredda had spent together in the Schultz home, as they came to understand how the lives of their families had become interwoven, then later as they cared for Tatiana and shared pieces of their hearts and their fears and sorrows, Fredda had taught Dagmar to sew lace. So when Rose assumed her mother had made this tablecloth, the truth was closer than she knew.

Jan's pulse started to pound in her temples as her fingers kept creeping over the surface of the lace. She didn't see anything else as she inched toward the final corner, increasing her pace with the hunch that if there was a picture in the lace, Dagmar would have put it in a corner, just as she'd put her signature in one.

Although she had no way of knowing for certain how everything had happened, Jan imagined the two young women working on the tablecloth over the weeks and months, nearly finishing it together. Then in the final hours before her arrest, while Fredda and Tatiana slumbered in their beds, Dagmar had figured out a way to let Fredda know where she'd hidden the valuable brooch.

If Fredda was questioned, Dagmar wanted her to be ignorant of where the brooch was. Fredda had already been accused once of stealing it. Berta Schultz would make her pay dearly if she was caught knowing where it was. Jan could almost see Dagmar awake late at night, as Jan was now, back hunched and neck aching as she worked over the tablecloth, sewing her love into every stitch.

Jan's fingers kept moving and her eyes kept searching. She reached the corner. And there it was. She could hardly breathe. Woven into the lace was a clear image of Beatrice, Rose's childhood doll.

She prayed that during their ransacking, the Tates had passed over that beautiful doll, where the brooch was almost certainly hidden.

By EIGHT O'CLOCK Wednesday morning, Clifton, Rose, Jan, and Elaine were picking their steps over the mess in the sitting room.

As they searched for the doll, Clifton and Rose looked stunned at seeing the house again in the daylight. Books were strewn everywhere and the furniture cushions torn, their stuffing billowing out. Upstairs, dresser drawers had been emptied, mattresses flipped, closets disheveled.

"They worked fast," Elaine said.

Everyone was amazed how much the Tates had undone in a few short minutes before they heard sirens wailing toward the house.

They gingerly stepped over the clutter, unable to keep from rescuing other things as they looked for Beatrice.

Jan had picked her way to the other side of the room, passing Clifton, who was brushing his fingers over the cracked glass of a family picture frame.

"Found her." Rose was straightening up by a corner window, and Beatrice was in her hand. The doll's curls and dress were tousled, and she had a small chip in the porcelain near her ear. But overall she could have fared much worse. And best of all, she was still there.

Rose seemed to look with new eyes. "Oh, look!" She pulled gently at something near Beatrice's neck and slowly withdrew a gold chain from beneath the bodice of the doll's dress. "My pendant!" she said on a breath.

They crowded around Rose while she undid the clasp and freed her childhood necklace.

Rose handed the necklace to her father, who fastened it around her neck.

Elaine tenderly touched the small figure eight at Rose's neck.

"It's so pretty, Rose," Jan said.

"It's a little small now," she said with a quick, teary laugh.

"I think it looks very delicate at your throat," Elaine assured her. "You could always add an extender."

Rose smoothed the doll's pinafore and held a tiny porcelain hand and touched the smoothness of one of the Mary Jane shoes. Then she began to look it over more intently as the others hovered close. After a minute she shrugged. "I don't see anything unusual," she said, handing the doll to Jan to take a look.

It was the perfect place, the favorite toy belonging to the child two mothers called daughter. With the others hovering over her, Jan ran her fingers slowly over the smoothness of the porcelain, feeling for the subtlest discrepancy in the workmanship. Fissures or lines in the paint that might camouflage a hiding place. She looked first at the doll's face and then lifted the ruffled dress and pinafore to look over the arms, the hands, the legs, and finally the tiny feet.

As she moved her fingers over the doll's right ankle, she felt something. It was an unevenness at the lower part of the leg, just above the sock. She lifted the foot to look more closely and saw a horizontal line that circled the doll's leg. It would have been almost impossible to recognize with only a passing look, but she could see that it had been glued. "This is it." She looked up at Rose. "Is it okay to crack it?"

"And after all Mom did to keep me from wrecking her as a kid..." But Rose looked animated instead of sad at the thought.

They looked around for something to use as a hammer.

"Here, use this." Clifton handed Jan a metal candle snuffer.

The first few taps did nothing. Jan shrugged off any guilt that she was about to destroy a family heirloom by reminding herself that doing so could mean big things for Rose and Clifton. She whacked the little leg harder. A chip broke off and skittered to the rug. She brought the snuffer down two more times, and the foot and ankle cracked away. She picked up the doll by the broken leg to peer inside the cavity.

"There's something inside." She wanted to reach into the leg but instead handed Beatrice back to Rose, who took her carefully. She slipped a slender finger into the leg and connected with something. With a few wiggles of her finger, bit by bit a curled-up piece of paper appeared. Rose pulled it out the rest of the way, the doll dropped backward, and something clinked inside of it as it hung by the leg.

Elaine took the paper and began to unfold it while Rose tipped the doll right side up and held her other hand under the broken leg. Something dropped into her palm.

They were looking at an antique gold brooch in a figure-eight design. Two large and still brilliant diamonds glistened in the loops.

CHAPTER TWENTY-FOUR

It was Wednesday night, more than a week since they'd found the jewelry inside Beatrice's leg and they'd learned of the arrests of Ray and Sabine Meyer. But tonight wasn't only a celebration of a recovered treasure. Tea for Two was hosting the victory celebration of Lancaster's newest selectman, Dr. Clifton Young. They'd finished the official vote count that morning.

Jan was putting the last touches on her makeup in her bathroom upstairs when she heard the front doorbell ring. She hurried downstairs and smiled to Bob on the other side of the door. He was early and she was glad. She welcomed him with a hug that lingered before she stepped back to let him come in.

The entry hall and parlors were adorned with victory banners, and the whole house smelled of hors d'oeuvres and pastries, punch, and of course, tea. Jan and Rose had made most of the food, but had also taken Clifton up on his offer to have the rest catered. A good choice, Jan thought again.

She'd chosen a shimmery pink sundress with a white bolero sweater and low white heels. Bob's expression told her she'd done well. He was wearing pumpkin-colored shorts with a white golf shirt that deepened his dark eyes and hair.

"Rose and Clifton are here already, and everyone else should arrive in a few minutes," she explained, leading the way to the east parlor. "I think we'll be okay on space since we've got the dining room back."

A truck from the Waterville food pantry had come earlier in the week to pick up the donations that were stacked almost to the ceiling in some places and had filled almost every inch of floor space. The room, as well as the town, had returned to summer-normal.

Brian and Paula were talking with the Youngs and Elaine when Jan and Bob entered the east parlor. She caught Paula's smile and knew her family had noticed that Bob was becoming a friendly fixture around the tearoom. Friends. That was all they officially were for now, but time would tell. Whatever it was at this moment, she was enjoying it.

Amy's family and Tara walked in without knocking a couple of minutes later. Everyone was dressed in nice summer outfits and smelling soapy fresh, while the feast laid out on four covered tables near the fireplace had the room smelling of stuffed mushrooms, bacon-wrapped figs, and mounds of skewered pork medallions and chicken fingers. The desserts had a table to themselves, and Jan's grandkids were already scoping out the cream puffs, flourless chocolate cakes, and mini cheesecakes.

A punch bowl and the tea urns were set up on the fourth table, along with cups, napkins, and clear plasticware. Two hours ago, she'd met a couple high school seniors who were on summer staff for the catering company. They'd keep the food and drinks flowing so Jan and Elaine could enjoy their guests.

Jan had wanted a few minutes with this group before the rest of the town showed up. She looked around at each one with a sense of fullness. Near the drink table, Bob talked easily with Brian and Clifton. Rose was showing Avery and Paula the diamond brooch that glistened on the lace shoulder scarf she'd put over her bright purple maxi dress. It was an interesting combination of old and new styles, but it worked for this special night.

The week had been a wonderful release after the days leading up to the election. Jan had harbored doubts that Clifton would pull it off, but the Youngs' troubles actually got people talking about the man who'd been a good neighbor and friend. He won the election by a respectable margin, and J. Eisley Segouri had made a brief concession speech for the local TV news with decent congratulations to Clifton.

Jan thought she heard the front doorbell ring again and waved to the others. "It's time!"

For the next twenty minutes, she lost track of how many times she opened the door to neighbors and friends who came in with smiling faces and hearty congratulations for their new town official. Jan had never had so many people in her home at one time. Two hundred visitors must have come and gone as the sun dropped over the western end of Chickadee Lake and birds quieted their twittering.

Lights went on in the tearoom entry hall, both parlors, and the private dining room.

"Isn't it fun all lit up?" Elaine commented to Jan with a hug. She looked attractive in a seafoam-colored A-line dress with lace overlay. Jan complimented her on it, and Elaine shrugged as she handed a cup of punch to Jan. "Thought I'd stick with the lace theme one more night."

Jan saw all four grandkids disappear up the stairs with plates of food, to eat in the tower room, she assumed. She gently elbowed her cousin, who was finishing a last bite of cream puff. "Lucky them that we found a place with its own pirate dungeon."

Elaine swallowed. "Don't let the girls hear you call it that. They claim it's their clubhouse, and something tells me they won't be ousted by two rug-rat boys."

Jan laughed as she licked a pouf of lime sherbet from her lip and took another sip of the green punch. "So I guess we're not really going to be featured in *Lakeside Lights* after all." She looked at Elaine. "We don't need some old magazine story to boost business, anyway," she joked.

"Nah. We're good," Elaine said, but Jan could see that Elaine had felt that same sense of disappointment she'd felt too. Perhaps they'd end up getting good press in another way, down the road.

As Clifton said a few words to the crowd, Jan mulled once more over the events of the past week. The Tates had been booked on several charges that should earn both of them a decent amount of jail time. Allie was given fifty hours of community service by local authorities. Clifton had actually helped Allie find a new place to rent near A Cut Above, and he was finding ways for her to complete her hours of service around town. Contrite and a little more matured through her mistakes, Allie had been to Tea for Two a couple of times in the past week. Jan had even seen Rose sit and chat with her for a few minutes when it was quiet.

Jan looked at the brooch shimmering on Rose's scarf again and thought of all the connections that had finally come together. The brooch, the tie tack, the pendant that had belonged to the Beck family. The three pieces had been as scattered as their original owners. It turned out that the brooch wasn't the only thing Dagmar had hidden in Beatrice's leg. The piece of rolled-up paper Rose had pulled out first was a copy of the custody document that left Rose in Fredda's care. After the brooch fell out, Rose stuck her pinkie into the alcove again and wiggled free a rolled-up letter from Dagmar.

Rose looked filled with wonder as she read her birth mother's words to her. Dagmar's script was firm and flowing. After a minute Rose read the letter, translating it for the others in English.

Dagmar wrote about the Beck and Schultz families, and how the pendant and the brooch that rightfully belonged to the Becks had ended up in the Schultz family...

... brooch, Tatiana. It belonged to Fredda's mother, and if you are reading this, then Fredda is now your second mother. She loves you as I do. After all, she has known you as long. While it is my greatest desire to see you grow up, if that does not happen, I know that Fredda will be the mother you need. She loves you and she loves the God who will guide and guard you every day of your life. His plans for you are good, mein Schatzi, and while your ancestors made some terrible mistakes, you are not bound by them. Trust God to lead you on the path He created for you. You have had my heart ever since I knew you were coming, and I pray I will see you again someday. Your loving Mutter.

CHAPTER TWENTY-FIVE

The moon was high in the sky outside the tearoom when the crowd finally thinned. Rose came over to give Elaine a hug, and only then did Elaine notice the bracelet Rose was wearing. "How...?"

"Lila gave it to me. I guess she inherited it through the family and knew it belonged to Dagmar. I got the clasp fixed so it won't fall off anymore." She reached up to touch the brooch. "I'm wearing something from each of my mothers tonight." Her blue eyes shone.

Rose slipped away to her father's side, and the doorbell rang again. Elaine saw with pleasant surprise that Thomas Spence was standing on the doorstep. He held his wallet in one hand and a small envelope in the other.

"Elaine, I didn't even realize until I was driving over here tonight that I ran off without paying you and Jan for the tea and muffins I took last week." He grinned sheepishly. "You must have thought me the worst sort of pastry thief."

"Well," Elaine said with a chuckle, "now that you mention it, yes, yes, we did! But put your wallet away please. You've done so much to help Rose. Please accept the goodies as a sincere token of our appreciation."

"Thank you. They were delicious, by the way."

"You're welcome." She paused, remembering Thomas's strange visit. "But I'm still puzzled why you came in that day."

Spence gave her a cryptic smile. "You know what they always say...'If I told you, then...'"

Elaine burst out laughing. "Let's not even go there."

"It was a ruse, really, so I could have a chance to ask you two, and more so Rose, some questions. But I was the one getting the third degree."

"And the free muffins," Elaine added with a grin.

Clifton must have seen Thomas enter, because he strode over at that moment to join them, followed by Rose and Jan. He reached out to shake hands with the man who'd done so much for his family.

"Clifton. Rose. I came to offer congratulations. And to bring you this." He handed a manila envelope to Rose.

She slipped a single piece of paper from it. She studied it for a moment, a wistful, faraway look in her eyes, before looking up to Thomas. "Tatiana Rose Schultz. My first birth certificate."

"And Bob says you should be getting your Rose Tatiana Sims American birth certificate soon, so you'll have a full set of identity papers," Jan told her with a misty smile.

Rose crossed the circle of people who cared about her and gave Thomas a hug.

A half hour later, Elaine closed the door after Thomas and turned around to see Nathan coming toward her.

"Nice party."

"Thanks. I think it went well. The town seems happy to have Clifton on board. Thanks for bringing Fredda's and Tatiana's death certificates back."

"Ah, it was no trouble."

"Have you got a busy week ahead?"

"Nothing too bad. I'm looking forward to waterskiing Sunday afternoon. Sure you're ready?" He was referring to Clifton's invitation for a longer boat outing that weekend.

Elaine hadn't convinced Jan yet to try getting up on skis, but she herself couldn't wait. "Ready as I'll ever be!"

After the last guests had left and the tearoom was quiet again, Elaine and Jan slipped off their shoes and headed back to the office, where Brian had pulled away from the party earlier to work some more on the walls.

He was standing on the ladder, gazing intently at the flue cover, but looked at his mother and Elaine when they came into the room.

"Thanks for working so hard on that, Bri." Jan smiled up at him.

"It's the least I can do. I'm almost done with the hard part. Mom, would you mind handing up my phone on the desk?"

She did, and he snapped a couple of pictures of the flue cover and handed the phone back to Jan. "What do you make of that?"

Together the cousins looked at the phone and then up at the plain, flat flue cover that no longer was covered with wallpaper.

"This cover has etchings, with texture," Brian said. "Someone had to have put them there on purpose. They're really primitive. Like they were kind of hastily scratched in?"

"It almost looks like...doesn't it remind you of some kind of crest?" Jan asked.

Elaine looked curiously at her cousin. "A family crest?"

"Uh-huh."

Elaine looked again at the markings on the wall, then back at Jan. "I can't think why anyone would take the time to carve a crest only to wallpaper over it."

"Unless whoever marked it knew it would be covered up and hidden from prying eyes," Jan countered.

"Could be. And maybe whoever stuck wallpaper over it didn't think anything of it." Then she looked at Jan. "Do you think it might have something to do with the ring?"

"And those marks on the ring box." Jan looked back, both confused and intrigued.

"You up for more investigating?"

Behind her glasses, Jan's eyes twinkled in anticipation. "I'm starting to think this mystery stuff is becoming a hobby."

Elaine smiled. "Who knew that Chickadee Lake would be such a hotbed of intrigue?"

ABOUT THE AUTHOR

Tea Rose is Erin Keeley Marshall's first published work of fiction with Guideposts, but she has also enjoyed contributing to the devotional book *Mornings with Jesus* since its beginning in 2012. She is the author of *Navigating Route 20-Something* and *The Daily God Book*, a collaborating writer for *365 Pocket Prayers for Mothers* and *Hope of Heaven: God's Eight Messages of Assurance to a Grieving Father*, and a contributing writer and editor for many other publications. Erin lives in Arkansas with her husband, Steve, and their kids, Paxton and Calianne. Visit her at erinkeeleymarshall.com and on Facebook and Twitter @EKMarshall.

GREAT-GREAT-AUNT ZELLA'S KRINGLAS

½ cup butter, softened

1¼ cup sugar

2 egg yolks

1 cup buttermilk

3 cups flour

1 teaspoon baking powder

½ teaspoon baking soda

½ teaspoon salt

½ to 1 teaspoon ground cardamom

Preheat oven to 350 degrees. Cream together the butter and sugar until light. Beat in the egg yolks. Blend in the buttermilk.

In a separate bowl, stir together the remaining ingredients. Blend into creamed mixture and beat well.

Divide dough in half. Wrap each half in plastic wrap, and place both halves in the freezer for two hours. Work with one half at a time, leaving the other half in the freezer until ready to use.

Divide each half into eighteen pieces. With floured hands, roll dough pieces on floured pastry cloth into seven-inch ropes. Handle dough as lightly as possible. It will be soft, so flour hands and surface often.

To shape, bring ends together, overlapping slightly. Twist once, forming a figure-eight. Place on lightly greased cookie sheet. Bake for twelve to fourteen minutes or until lightly browned on the bottom (tops will be pale). Repeat with remaining dough.

Read on for an exciting sneak peek
into the next volume of Tearoom Mysteries!

To a Tea
by Vera Dodge

Elaine Cook felt like a queen.

She was sitting on the porch of a big, rambling Victorian house, overlooking the beautiful waters of Chickadee Lake. She had a cup of some of the finest tea in the world by her side, hand-crafted of petals and spices by a Persian woman in upstate New York. The sun was shining brightly on the blue waters under the August sky, as if the weather was putting on a command performance just for her.

Who else but a queen would be able to live so well?

And Elaine even had some queenly business to attend to.

On her lap sat a stack of applications for employment at Tea for Two.

Rose, their first hire, had done a wonderful job so far. But the business that Elaine and her cousin Jan had started in the beautiful old home was growing.

For the time being, she and Rose and Jan could handle the demand from the customers who came each day for the peaceful respite Tea for Two offered from the stress and bustle of the rest of the world. And so far, they'd also been able to field all of the celebration tea parties and special events that their guests had requested—barely.

But Jan and Elaine hadn't opened the tearoom because they wanted to make a lot of money or have more to do. They'd opened it because they loved the quiet pleasure of taking some time to deeply enjoy something as simple as a cup of tea themselves. And at this pace, they hardly ever got a chance to take a day off—or even just sit down.

So it was time to hire someone else.

And after that, Elaine thought, glancing at a second folder that she had left on the low table beside the wicker chair where she sat, she had a treat to look forward to. Felicia Standish would arrive in a few minutes—Tea for Two's very first bride.

Booking a wedding at Tea for Two so soon after they'd opened was a coup. But what meant much more to Elaine was the relationship she had developed with Felicia over the past several weeks.

Felicia had actually started to visit the tearoom with the stacks of books and binders that all modern brides seemed to cart around these days, spending afternoon after afternoon poring through them, a worried look on her face.

Elaine had recognized it immediately, although she and her late husband, Ben, had gotten married years ago in a much simpler ceremony, which Elaine's mother had mostly planned. Elaine had never been sure she liked not having much say in her own wedding. But when she looked at the worried faces of modern brides, who seemed to feel required now to put on something like a Vegas floor show, not just a wedding, Elaine sometimes felt grateful for the simplicity of her own ceremony.

Still, there was something undeniably exciting about putting together a memorable day, with every detail just right.

Elaine knew some of that thrill from all the work she and Jan had put into the thoughtful details at Tea for Two, from the charming pieces of mismatched china that each of them had painstakingly chosen from the shelves of local thrift stores and flea markets, to the collection of Nanking teapots that their grandmother had collected years ago, which they now proudly displayed in the west parlor.

So when Felicia chose Tea for Two as her ground zero for wedding planning, Elaine had approached her with both tea and sympathy.

Maybe it was Elaine's listening ear. Or maybe it was just the tea. But in any case, Felicia quickly opened up to Elaine about her trials with the wedding.

She'd found the perfect dress, and a neighbor had planted flowers that spring that she should be able to harvest into beautiful bouquets by late August, when the wedding was planned.

But she was having a terrible time finding a venue.

She and Ryan had been dating for years, first as high school sweethearts, and then while he'd been deployed as a soldier overseas. So when he finally returned to his hometown and proposed that spring, neither of them wanted to wait any longer than they had to. So they'd set the date in August.

"But every place in town is already booked!" Felicia had told Elaine. "I even thought about renting out one of those big fishing boats that sometimes take out party tours. Even the fishing boats are booked!"

That's when the idea had formed in Elaine's mind. She and Jan had talked about possibly doing weddings at Tea for Two. But neither of them had felt that they had the resources to get the basic tearoom up and running, and also handle all the stress of preparations for summer weddings—at least not during their very first summer in business.

But Elaine hadn't been able to resist the look on Felicia's face. And to tell the truth, the tearoom was running well enough that she was itching to try something new.

So finally she'd broached the idea to Jan.

When she did, Jan got a funny look on her face.

"It's strange you're bringing that up now," she said.

"Oh?" Elaine had asked her. "Why's that?"

"Because I just had a talk with Ryan's mother, Willa," Jan said. "I know her through the painting class I've been taking. She told me that Ryan and Felicia wanted to get married here."

"Maybe it's a sign we're supposed to have them as our first wedding," Elaine said.

"I'm not sure I'd go that far," Jan said. "But if you feel strongly about it, I could be convinced."

The next time Felicia came into the shop to plan, Elaine had listened to her talk about her progress on planning—and her lack of progress in finding a venue—for a few minutes.

"Well," Elaine had said then, "how do you like this place?"

"This place?" Felicia had looked around. "Actually, it's perfect. I love it here. You can tell that from how often I come in. But you don't do weddings—" Her eyes widened. "Do you?"

It had taken Elaine a day to find a contract on the Internet that would cover the event. Felicia signed it, joyfully, the next morning.

Ever since then, the two of them had been meeting together to talk about all the details of the wedding. And over time, the conversations had turned to questions of marriage—Felicia's hopes and dreams and questions about what it would really mean, not just to be a bride, but to be a wife.

Elaine was glad to have those conversations. In some ways they were bittersweet for her, because they brought up the fresh loss of her husband, Ben, whose death had been so unexpected. But it was also a lovely way to remember him.

Elaine wasn't the kind to sit around thinking over old memories. She was the kind to move back to Maine and start a new business. But she didn't mind sharing what she knew about marriage with Felicia, especially if the wisdom she and Ben had gained in their time together might help the young couple thrive in their early years.

And it turned out that talking with Felicia about her marriage actually warmed Elaine's own heart.

So Elaine was almost as excited as Felicia was for the big day, which was now only a week away. And Elaine was looking forward to tacking down some of the last details—which included tasting a suite of truffles that would be wrapped in beautiful tulle and ribbon as the hostess gifts. She'd had to restrain herself from breaking into the box and taking a taste of the delicious treats all morning.

In the meantime, though, she still had a task at hand: finding more hands—or really, more willing hearts—to help out with Tea for Two's growing business

Elaine pored over each of the dozen or so applications, really trying to get a feel for what each person was like.

But one caught Elaine's eye.

First of all, it was from a man, Archie Bentham.

Second, he had a degree from Oxford. And another one from Cambridge.

And, as Elaine read down the page, she discovered that he had lived all over the world: Latin America, South Africa, even Japan. Apparently, he'd started businesses of some kind in all of them. Oil. Real Estate. Construction.

There didn't seem to be anywhere that Archie Bentham hadn't been.

Or anything he couldn't do.

"So why in the world," Elaine wondered out loud to Earl Grey, "would he want to work here at our little tearoom?"

Earl Grey seemed to give his attention to this question, staring back into Elaine's eyes for a long moment.

But then he flopped over onto the porch, as if he'd considered the whole thing, and didn't find anything in it worth getting too riled up over.

Elaine had always loved this about Earl Grey. Unlike other cats, he never pretended to ignore your existence. But at the same time, he never seemed to let very much upset him. And his placid attitude was often a good reminder to her not to let herself get carried away wondering or worrying about the small stuff.

Still, she couldn't help being curious about this Archie Bentham. And the fact that apparently he wanted the next line on his extraordinary résumé to read "Tea for Two."

She laid his application to the side, and then continued through the stack. When she reached the bottom, she'd discarded the ones that didn't seem like a good fit: a few young people who didn't plan to be in the area for long enough to make it worthwhile to train them; a few who didn't seem to have any relevant experience; and a few she just didn't feel a connection with.

That left three. One was an older woman who was looking to pick up part-time hours, and wrote that she had been throwing tea parties for her friends, and then her children, and now her grandchildren, all her life.

She might fit right in with Jan and me, Elaine thought.

One was a local high school student. She was young, but she had good grades, and she would be in town for several more years. So she and Jan could really teach and shape her, Elaine thought. Elaine loved her growing connection with Jan's grandchildren, who lived in nearby Augusta. And it could be lovely to have some more young people around. *Who knows?* she thought. *This one might even help bring the delight of good tea to a whole new generation in Lancaster.*

But when she stacked the two of them together, she couldn't resist looking back at Archie Bentham's application, which still sat on the table apart from all the rest.

It should have been easy to dismiss. He was so obviously overqualified for the tearoom.

But something, maybe her curiosity, wouldn't quite let go.

With a sigh, Elaine picked up the page Archie Bentham had filled out and placed it with the résumés of the two other applicants she intended to interview.

Her face hovered between a smile and a frown as she did: the frown, because she wasn't sure exactly why she couldn't just let the application go into the pile with the others who wouldn't be getting a call. And the smile out of amusement at herself.

"I thought you were the one who was supposed to be curious," she told Earl Grey.

Earl Grey just flicked his tail.

"Well," Elaine said, "I know one thing. There's a good chance this will be an interesting interview."

Earl Grey tilted his head, with a slight show of interest.

"And maybe that's a good enough reason," Elaine said, reaching for her phone. "After all, not everything in the world has to be about just getting things done. Sometimes it's all right to just enjoy all the wonder in the world. Isn't that the whole point of a tea shop?"

The whole point of the tea shop, as far as Earl Grey seemed to understand, was to provide him a shady porch on which to loll during the heat of a beautiful summer day.

Elaine dialed Archie Bentham's number.

Almost on the first ring, a clipped Englishman's voice with a posh accent answered. "Hello?"

"This is Elaine Cook," she told him. "I'm trying to reach Archie Bentham."

Something told her she'd already reached him, and the posh English voice quickly confirmed it. "Why yes," he said. "I'm afraid that's me. And I'm delighted to hear from you!"

"It was something of a surprise to receive your application," Elaine told him. "I don't think we had any other applicants who have also built luxury hotels on the Arabian Peninsula."

"You won't hold that against me, will you?" Archie asked.

Elaine smiled. It was hard to hold anything against someone with that kind of an accent. Especially since she'd spent so many years studying the history of tea, and the English contributions to the ancient ritual of tea ceremonies.

She still assumed she wasn't going to hire him. But that didn't mean she wouldn't enjoy a good conversation with him.

She laughed. "No," she said. "But I would like to hear a bit more about how Tea for Two fits into your career plan."

"Well, that's a very interesting story," Archie said. "And I'd love to tell it to you, if you have the time."

"That sounds lovely," Elaine said.

They negotiated for a few moments before settling on a time to meet the next day.

"I'm looking forward to it," Elaine said.

"As am I," Archie said. Then his voice turned serious. "All joking aside," he said, "I want you to know that nobody in the world could be more serious about tea than I."

Elaine knew that he was just trying to indicate how serious he was about the job. But something about what he'd said, and the way he said it, rankled her. Of course this Englishman thought he knew more about tea than anyone else in the world. But the English didn't have the monopoly on caring about tea.

Elaine had spent years of her life learning about tea, and enjoying it, herself.

Still, Archie went on, his voice strangely humble, in contrast to the quick wit and confidence with which he'd started the call. "Truly," he said. "I know it must have come as an unusual application. And I'm very grateful to you for even considering it. I can't imagine work I'd enjoy more."

"Not even reopening a grand marina on the Brazilian coast?" Elaine asked, picking one of the details off his résumé at random.

"There are a lot of things in this world that sound quite a bit more romantic than they are," Archie said. "And in my experience, Brazilian marinas are one of them." He sighed. "When you've done as much traveling as I have, sometimes all the magnificent places blend together. And all you want is something that seems like home."

This, Elaine could actually relate to. "I know what you mean," she said. "I've traveled a lot in my life too."

"I'll look forward to hearing all about it," Archie said.

Elaine rang off, and picked up the other applications to call another candidate.

But before she could punch the next number into her phone, she heard a footstep on the porch.

When she looked up, Felicia was rounding the corner.

This was an event that Earl Grey seemed to think was important enough to warrant getting up for. He hopped to his feet and headed straight for her, his bushy gray tail waving a greeting and accompanied by several celebratory mews.

Elaine couldn't blame him. Felicia was a beautiful girl, with thick curly red hair that fell past her shoulders, and blue eyes set in a porcelain face dusted with cinnamon freckles. But the cat was probably responding to her inner beauty—a kind of quiet kindness, combined with a mischievous sparkle in her eye—that was far more attractive than her physical beauty, both to people and cats, who loved to crowd around her, not because of how she looked, but who she was.

As Felicia bent down to scratch Earl Grey's ears, Elaine checked the time. Had she let the morning get away from her? She hadn't expected to see Felicia for another hour, at least.

But the phone told her that it was about the time she had thought. It was Felicia who was impressively early.

Elaine laid her applications for employment aside with a sigh. You could never how tell how being a bride was going to affect somebody. The nerves did strange things to every woman Elaine had ever seen go through a wedding.

And if showing up a little too early was the worst of it, they were doing pretty well.

"I guess you just couldn't wait to try the truffles," Elaine said, standing up to go into the kitchen and retrieve the treats they'd planned to sample. "And it's probably a good thing you got here early. If you waited any longer, I might have eaten them all myself."

She expected Felicia to look up with her usual ready smile, but to her surprise, Felicia just kept petting Earl Grey, her head bowed over the soft ball of fur. Elaine might have thought that Felicia hadn't heard her at all, if it weren't for a slight jerk of Felicia's head as Elaine spoke.

"Felicia?" Elaine asked. "Is everything all right?"

When Felicia still failed to answer, Elaine knew that everything wasn't all right.

She took a deep breath. Felicia had been such a dream bride up to this point that Elaine had gotten spoiled, she told herself. But this was the last week before the wedding. It was natural that Felicia would be struggling with some deep emotions by this point. In fact, it was only surprising that she hadn't seemed to struggle more up till now.

But whatever it was, Elaine thought, she'd probably heard it before. Between Jan's marriage, and her own son's marriage, and her marriage to Ben, and all the stories she'd heard from her other dear friends, there wasn't much that would surprise her.

She was just glad that she had the chance to be there for Felicia at this moment, because she knew enough about Felicia and Ryan's relationship to believe that they were going to make it. They had a solid foundation: a long friendship and a realistic view of what a strong marriage was really going to take. They weren't just two kids who had fallen for each other in the heat of youthful passion. Their love had been tested by the years Ryan spent away. If they didn't have a real friendship and a deep commitment, they wouldn't have made it.

So whatever was happening now must be some kind of misunderstanding, some small conflict that they'd just need to face together on the way to the altar, as they'd need to face other obstacles together throughout the rest of their lives.

But, Elaine knew, whatever was going on might still sting in the short term.

So she leaned down and patted Felicia's shoulder. "Hey, honey," she said. "It's all right. What's going on?"

When Elaine touched Felicia's shoulder, Felicia finally looked up. Elaine could see that her big blue eyes were full of tears, which had already started to slide down her face.

"Hey," Elaine said, putting an arm around Felicia's shoulders, "whatever it is, it can't be that bad. The two of you will get through this together. I know it."

For some reason, this didn't seem to comfort Felicia at all. Instead of calming down, she gave a broken sob. Then she wrapped her arms around Elaine, clinging as if for dear life as she wept and struggled to catch her breath.

Elaine patted her back with increasing alarm. Some nerves were normal, but Felicia seemed truly brokenhearted. And she had never been one for drama, at least since Elaine had known her.

Had something gone terribly wrong?

"Felicia," Elaine said. "Honey. Can you tell me what's happening? Is it something I can help you with?"

Finally, Felicia pulled back and looked Elaine in the eyes.

For a long moment, she seemed to have lost the power of speech.

But eventually she found the words and managed to get them out.

"It's Ryan," she said. "He's gone."

FROM THE
GUIDEPOSTS ARCHIVES

This story, by Keri Wolf of Golden, Colorado, originally appeared in the December 1990 edition of *Guideposts*.

For a good deal of my twenty-six years, a part of me wondered who I was. Not that I didn't know my name, or where I lived, or what I believed in. You see, I am an adopted child, and I always felt a piece of the puzzle was missing. Not all adopted kids feel this way. Many have no desire to dig up the past. For me, though, it was a question that gnawed at me all through my growing-up years. Something told me—something insistent and powerful inside—that I was one of those children meant to reunite with her birth mother.

Yet it took me a long time to begin that search, and it wasn't until it was over that I understood that I had been guided all along.

Here's what I knew about my past: I was born in Winona, Minnesota, given up for adoption as an infant and taken to Nebraska. My adoptive parents never hid the fact that I was not biologically theirs. I sometimes wondered if it was that knowledge that made me develop such a tough streak of strong-willed independence. At a young age I struck out on my own.

That tough veneer began to fade a little as I drifted from job to job, town to town, never quite knowing where I was going next or what I wanted from life. Through the years my longing for my biological mother never weakened, but I always told myself that it would have to wait until I got my life settled.

Eventually I ended up in Golden, a friendly little town nestled at the foot of the soaring Rocky Mountains. I loved it; the town felt right. I found a job at the local Dairy Queen, which was great because I loved working with the public. It was a neat way to meet people. One day during the lunch rush a young man approached the counter to order a burger and fries. I looked up to ask about a drink order, and suddenly I was met with the most beautiful eyes I'd ever seen, as clear and as blue as the crystal Colorado sky.

"I guess I'll take a Coke," he said quietly. Don't ask me how, but suddenly I knew I'd just met the man I would marry.

Virgil and I did get married. With Virgil's support, I began thinking seriously about finding my natural mother. There is something very scary about facing the unknown. You never know what you'll find. Every time I steeled myself to pick up the phone and make that first call back to the hospital in Winona, my nerve failed me. I'd put it off for another day.

Finally the time came when I couldn't put it off any longer. I knew I would have to make a decision, a decision that might change my life forever. That morning I got up and dressed for work as usual. But I took an extra moment to say a prayer that my grandma back in Nebraska had taught me as a child. It was a prayer that had always helped me feel protected, secure, especially during my years of wandering: I need You, God. Please be with me today.

I put off the call all morning until the lunch rush made it impossible for me to have a break. As I was waiting to take the order from the next person in line, a piece of paper slid across the counter. "Hot dog and onion rings," it said in neat script. For an instant I was puzzled, then I looked up to see one of my regulars, Merle, a deaf man. I was glad to see him; he'd been away for a while. My spirits lifted every time Merle came in. He had even been teaching me sign language.

"No," I mouthed deliberately, shaking my head and smiling teasingly, "sign your order to me."

Merle grinned as if to say, You're right! He put his fist to his eyes like he was crying. *Onions*, of course. He made a circle with his thumb and index finger—ring. He pointed to a sign advertising hot dogs. Laughing, I gave him the thumbs-up sign and put his order in.

"Come back soon," I signed as he waved good-bye.

Merle was just the boost I needed that day. As soon as my break came I got on the pay phone in back. I steadied my fingers and dialed.

"Hello?" I fairly shouted at the voice answering on the other end. "I was born at your hospital twenty-three years ago. I'm looking for my birth mother. I'm adopted."

The information spilled out of me. "Hold on, young lady," came the reply. "Let me give you the number of someone who can help."

The people I talked with at the Minnesota Adoption Unit were very nice but not necessarily encouraging. I guess I'd been naive. There was a lot more to finding my mother than merely picking up the phone and asking. Records and documents would have to be requested in writing; there seemed to be hundreds of forms to fill out, questionnaires to answer. Then there was the original birth certificate. It could not be released to me without my birth mother's consent. This would have to be her decision as well as mine.

"We will conduct a six-month search," a woman at the Adoption Unit explained one day over the phone. "If she can be located and gives her permission, we will forward the information to you."

As the days passed, doubts filled my mind. What if they can't find her? What if she doesn't want to see me? What if she doesn't care? I was drowning in what ifs. It reminded me of the insecurity of my days before Golden, before the Dairy Queen and Virgil. Again I reached for my prayer and hung on to it tighter than ever. I need You, God. Please be with me today.

Day after day I kept my mind occupied at work, chatting with the regulars and practicing my sign language whenever Merle came in.

Late one Friday afternoon an official-looking envelope arrived from the Minnesota Adoption Unit. Hands trembling, I tore open the letter. "We have been in contact with your birth mother," it said. "She would be interested in establishing contact if you so desire. She consents to release your birth certificate, but under state law we must wait one hundred twenty-one days." I felt my whole being sag. "Call if you so desire."

Desire I surely did, but it would have to wait until Monday morning. By now everything was closed back in Minnesota.

It was the worst wait of all. I felt each minute of the weekend crawl by. "Hang on, Keri," Virgil grinned. "This was meant to be. I feel it."

Finally Monday arrived. During the first lull in business at the Dairy Queen I rushed in back and pounced on the telephone.

"Do I really have to wait a hundred and twenty-one days to find out anything about her?" I demanded excitedly.

"No," the woman on the other end replied gently. "That's just for the official release. Do you want some information now?"

For an instant everything froze in time. A surge of raw emotion overcame me. I was on the threshold of discovering what I had ached to know for as long as I could remember. Events from my life flashed before me, all those times I'd cried and wondered and prayed. It was all coming to an end. I was almost doubled over with nervousness.

"Yes!" I exclaimed, groping for something to write with. "Tell me."

"Her name is Rosemary Savoy," she began as I scribbled down the information on the back of an order pad. "She lives in an apartment in Winona. She is fifty-four years old, medium height, long gray hair, blue eyes, and has never been married. She is friendly but very strong-willed . . ."

"Sounds familiar," I whispered.

"Excuse me?"

"Never mind . . ."

The woman told me some more things about my mother, interesting things, and gave me an address where I could write. "Good luck, Keri," she said warmly before hanging up. "I have a feeling things will work out fine between you two."

Mom and I exchanged letters and pictures. In one letter Mom wrote, "For a long time I cried for you. I prayed you were safe. I hoped I would find you again."

Those words rolled over me like a wave of love. She had never forgotten about me, just as I had never stopped thinking of her.

One warm day in April, Virgil and I drove out to the airport to meet my birth mother for the first time. As we parked the car and headed for the terminal where the plane from Minneapolis would arrive, I felt my stomach twisting and churning with excitement. This was it. The day I'd waited for all my life. *I need You, God. Please be with me today.*

I could have picked her out even without the picture. She seemed a bit rumpled and tired out by the long flight. But her eyes gleamed with recognition, looking me up and down, looking right through me almost, inside my heart.

I raised my hands in front of me in a gesture God had been preparing me for without my knowing why. You see, there was something else I had found out: Mom was deaf.

We came closer. Carefully, my hands spoke the one beautiful word I'd longed to speak. "Mother."

A NOTE FROM THE EDITORS

We hope you enjoyed Tearoom Mysteries, created by the Books and Inspirational Media Division of Guideposts, a nonprofit organization that touches millions of lives every day through products and services that inspire, encourage, help you grow in your faith, and celebrate God's love.

Thank you for making a difference with your purchase of this book, which helps fund our many outreach programs to military personnel, prisons, hospitals, nursing homes, and educational institutions.

We also create many useful and uplifting online resources. Visit Guideposts.org to read true stories of hope and inspiration, access OurPrayer network, sign up for free newsletters, download free e-books, join our Facebook community, and follow our stimulating blogs.

To learn about other Guideposts publications, including the best-selling devotional *Daily Guideposts*, go to ShopGuideposts.org, call (800) 932-2145, or write to Guideposts, PO Box 5815, Harlan, Iowa 51593.

Sign up for the
Guideposts Fiction Newsletter
and stay up-to-date on
the fiction you love!

You'll get sneak peeks of new releases, recommendations from other Guideposts readers, and special offers just for you . . .

And it's FREE!

Just go to Guideposts.org/newsletters
today to sign up.

Visit ShopGuideposts.org
or call (800) 932-2145

Find more inspiring fiction in these best-loved Guideposts series!

Sugarcreek Amish Mysteries

Be intrigued by the suspense and joyful "aha" moments in these delightful stories. Each book in the series brings together two women of vastly different backgrounds and traditions, who realize there's much more to the "simple life" than meets the eye.

Miracles of Marble Cove

Follow four women who are drawn together to face life's challenges, support one another in faith, and experience God's amazing grace as they encounter mysterious events in the small town of Marble Cove.

Secrets of Mary's Bookshop

Delve into a cozy mystery where Mary, the owner of Mary's Mystery Bookshop, finds herself using sleuthing skills that she didn't realize she had. There are quirky characters and lots of unexpected twists and turns.

Patchwork Mysteries

Discover that life's little mysteries often have a common thread in a series where every novel contains an intriguing mystery centered around a quilt located in a beautiful New England town.

Mysteries of Silver Peak

Escape to the historic mining town of Silver Peak, Colorado, and discover how one woman's love of antiques helps her solve mysteries buried deep in the town's checkered past.

**To learn more about these books,
visit ShopGuideposts.org**